My voice stalls. The̶ ̶ ̶s̶o̶m̶e̶t̶h̶i̶n̶g̶ ̶my brain's
been trying to ignore because it's impossible. It
d̶a̶w̶ned the moment I saw those antique desks,
t̶h̶ gaunt, pasty faces, and it was boosted by
   ̶i̶ngton's joke about the ration. I swallow
    but my words still come out as a croak.
'̶Wh *year* is this?'

  C̶ sy leers at me. 'It's nineteen fifty-two. Don't
  ̶s̶ay ̶y̶ou're going to claim you've been sent a year
e̶ arl̶y̶ you were meant to come next year?'

  I ̶h̶ardly hear her. There's a noise in my skull
li̶ ̶ ̶t̶ ̶e̶ sea̶ and my heart's pounding my ribs . . .

www.kidsatrandomhouse.co.uk

From the Carnegie Medal-winning author

ROBERT SWINDELLS

In the Nick of Time

CORGI YEARLING BOOKS

IN THE NICK OF TIME
A CORGI BOOK 978 0 552 55585 2

First published in Great Britain by Corgi Yearling Books,
an imprint of Random House Children's Books

Corgi edition published 2007

1 3 5 7 9 10 8 6 4 2

Copyright © Robert Swindells, 2007

Papers used by Random House Children's Books are natural,
recyclable products made from wood grown in sustainable forests.
The manufacturing processes conform to the environmental regulations
of the country of origin.

Set in 12/16pt Century Old Style
by Falcon Oast Graphic Art Ltd.

Corgi Books are published by Random House Children's Books,
61–63 Uxbridge Road, London W5 5SA,
a division of The Random House Group Ltd,
in Australia by Random House Australia (Pty) Ltd,
20 Alfred Street, Milsons Point, Sydney, NSW 2061, Australia,
in New Zealand by Random House New Zealand Ltd,
18 Poland Road, Glenfield, Auckland 10, New Zealand
in South Africa by Random House (Pty) Ltd,
Isle of Houghton, Corner of Boundary and Carse O'Gowrie Roads,
Houghton 2198, South Africa
and in India by Random House India Pvt Ltd,
301 World Trade Tower, Hotel Intercontinental Grand Complex,
Barakhamba Lane, New Delhi 110 001, India

THE RANDOM HOUSE GROUP Limited Reg. No. 954009

www.kidsatrandomhouse.co.uk

A CIP catalogue record for this book is available from the British Library.

Printed and bound in Great Britain by
Cox & Wyman Ltd, Reading, Berkshire

To everybody I love – especially you

A TRUE STORY

Once, about a hundred years ago, thousands of children were living in dark, overcrowded houses with rats and horrible smells and hardly anything to eat. No sunlight ever reached the streets these children played on; no grass grew in the cracks between broken flags and greasy cobbles. They knew nothing of flowers, birds or butterflies. They were so thin, these children, so pale and weak and hungry that many of them died, and those who lived grew up frail and crooked, with rotten teeth and hacking coughs.

One day, a group of doctors came up with an idea. 'These children need to get away from their

1

smelly houses,' they said. 'And those murky streets. They need fresh air and sunlight and nourishing food. Why don't we build a school, out in the country, with classrooms that have no walls, and bedrooms with big open windows, and desks you can carry outside in fine weather?'

People thought those doctors were crazy. 'No *walls*?' they hooted. 'What about when it rains? Snows? What happens when it's blowing a gale, or there's a hard frost? These children are sick already: make 'em sit in classrooms with no walls and they'll just die.'

'No they won't!' cried the doctors. 'Children're tougher than you think. We'll feed 'em up, give 'em warm coats and boots and gloves. They'll brush the snow off their desks and get on with their work, you'll see.'

So the school was built, and a bunch of children was sent to live there. To most people's surprise, they didn't die. In fact they got fit and strong, with rosy cheeks. A few ran away because they were homesick, but most of them thought it was a great life, eating jam roly-poly and writing essays while snow piled up on the teacher's desk.

Soon, more and more open air schools were

built. More and more poor children were sent to them, and fewer and fewer grew up weak and coughing. The schools kept going for ninety years or more, till all the dark little houses had been knocked down and even poor people had sunlight and better food to eat.

They're gone now, the open air schools. Gone, but not forgotten by the last of their pupils, who have lived to grow old, thanks to a crazy idea that wasn't so crazy after all.

CHAPTER ONE

A December morning, furred with frost. On iron ground, two people walk hand in hand, trailing plumes of breath through black bare trees. They are an old man and a girl of seven. Layers of clothing make their bodies shapeless, their movements stiff. The child speaks.

'There's nothing, Grandad. The birds have flown away, the squirrels and the flowers are asleep. What is there to look at in the woods?'

The old man gives the little hand a squeeze. 'We're in the midst of wonders, Charlotte, even on a day like today.' He smiles. 'It's a matter of knowing where to look.'

They come to an ice-bound pond, fringed with brittle stems of dead grasses. They stop. The little girl stares at the grey ice, the black leaves trapped inside it. Nothing can move.

The old man looks down at his granddaughter. 'Seems lifeless, Charlotte, doesn't it?'

The child nods, shivers. Stiffly her grandfather squats, hooks the fingers of both hands round the edge of a large flat stone, looks up with eyes that twinkle. 'Are you ready, Charlotte? Watch.'

Gently, he lifts the stone. In the soft mud underneath, where frost can't penetrate, four crested newts lie sleeping. The child gazes, enthralled, breathes, 'What are they *doing*, Grandad: are they all right?'

The old man chuckles. 'They're hibernating, Charlotte, and they'll be absolutely fine till spring, when they'll wake up and fill the pond with brand new tadpoles.' Carefully he lowers the stone, straightens up with difficulty.

'Wonders, Charlotte. All around, all the time.' He smiles, takes her hand. 'Come on: Grandma'll have the breakfast on by now.'

CHAPTER TWO

I'm Charlie and I'm twelve. There's me, my nine-year-old brother Acton and our spaniel, Keeper. Oh, and Mum and Dad. I don't like school, and my hobbies are talking to friends on my moby and listening to music.

Monday morning of half term I'm in my room with a CD on when I hear Mum at the foot of the stairs.

'Charlotte?'

'What?' I sigh, knowing it'll be *turn that music down*, as usual, but it isn't.

'Grandma phoned. They've taken Grandad into hospital again. Dad and I are going over to sit with her for a while. D'you want to come?'

'No.'

'I'm sure she'd love to see you.'

'No, Mum, I can't.'

'Can't? What does *that* mean?'

'Means I can't, that's all.' I'll get *selfish* again, not to mention *moody* and *sulky*, but it isn't that. It's because I'm scared. My grandad's dying and they think I don't know. Think I'm too young to handle the truth. They keep banging on about *when Grandad's better. When Grandad's better we'll all go away on holiday together.* Yeah, and pigs'll fly, right?

We're close, Grandad and me. Always have been. He's not like other grown-ups. He doesn't talk down to me because I'm a kid, he assumes I'm an intelligent human being. Even when I was two he'd be like, *what d'you say to a gentle stroll down the path with an old man, Charlotte?* He gave me my full name before I grew into it, would've stuck needles in his eyes before using baby-talk, and he always listens properly when I'm telling him something. I guess what I'm trying to say is, Grandad and I respect each other.

And it isn't as if I need to be told. You've only to look at Grandma's eyes, the way the light's gone out of them. And that's why I don't want to go. I can't stand to look at Grandma's eyes, but I won't say that to Mum.

She takes my brother instead, which means I can meet Pip without having to drag him along. Pip's my best friend. If anybody can help me forget about Grandad for a while, it's her.

I call her. I don't know it, but it won't be long before I'll be wishing I'd gone to Grandma's.

CHAPTER THREE

We slog uphill to Cold Tarn Woods. Not many people come here unless the tarn is frozen over and they can skate. It's February but there's no ice: global warming, I suppose.

Pip hacks at the leafmould with the toe of her trainer. 'So what's he actually *got*, your grandad?'

'Some sort of cancer. I think it's in – you know, a part you don't mention.'

'Uh-huh. And it's doing your head in?'

'Yeah, well: I've always got on great with him, see? He's not like other old people: he's interested, keeps up with what's happening. You can have a conversation with him.'

'I know what you mean. My grandma and grandad don't know what I'm on about half the time. They're like, *iPod: what the heck's iPod?* It's as if they've already resigned from the world.' She stops, snatches at the sleeve of my jacket. 'Hey, look.'

We've come to where the trees thin out, giving way to a flattish area where gorse and bracken grow. I don't think I've ever seen it in winter before. The bracken's died back, and there's a big oblong of old concrete that must be hidden most of the year. We go over to it and I probe a crumbling edge with my toe. 'What d'you think it is?'

Pip shrugs. 'It's just a slab of cement now, but I suppose it was a floor at one time.'

'Floor of *what*, right up here?'

'Dunno. Army camp maybe. Scout camp. Holiday camp. Look: there's another over there, and another.'

We walk about, hacking at dead vegetation and peering into gorse bushes, and it turns out there's lots of floors, if that's what they are. Six at least. Most are the same size, but we find a couple that're bigger, square instead of oblong. I try to remember if I've ever heard anyone mention a camp up here, but I don't think I have.

'Look.' Pip's found another but I've seen something else: a pathway like a line of stepping stones, almost buried. I start to walk along it but there are gaps, like some stones are missing. I need big strides, even jumps. Landing after a long jump my foot skids on green slime and I fall, slashing my cheek on gorse. I wince, screw up my eyes against the sting.

When I open them and blink away tears, I'm lying on mown grass, surrounded by long, low buildings. There's no gorse, no pathway, no sign of Pip. Gripped by sudden dread, I scramble to my feet, glancing wildly around, seeing nothing I recognize. I start to sob; I can't help it, I must've gone mad or something. Hearing somebody behind me I whirl, hoping it's Pip, seeing instead a middle-aged woman who smiles and says, 'You must be Joyce Ingham, we've been expecting you.'

CHAPTER FOUR

'Mrs Livingstone—'

'Pip, is that you? Whatever's the matter, you sound—'

'It's Charlie, Mrs Livingstone, she's disappeared. I'm up by Cold Tarn Woods. She's just vanished.'

'Vanished? What d'you mean, vanished? People don't—'

'But she *has*, Mrs Livingstone, I've looked everywhere. There's these old floors, cement floors, and I called to Charlie and when she didn't answer I turned round and she'd gone. I've even tried phoning.'

'D'you think . . . might she be playing a trick on you: hiding somewhere?'

'There's nowhere to hide, Mrs Livingstone. I mean, there's the woods but she couldn't have reached them, not in the time.'

'There aren't holes, are there? Cellars, drains? She hasn't knocked herself out or . . . ?'

'No, there's nothing like that, I've looked. I don't know what else to do.'

'Neither do I, Pip, to be perfectly honest. I mean, I don't want to get the police out, then find it's some sort of joke.'

'It's not a joke, Mrs Livingstone, I promise you that. I'm really, really scared.'

'All right, Pip, listen. Stay there, keep searching. I'm going to call the police, leave Acton with a neighbour and drive up. I'll be there as soon as I can, OK?'

'OK, Mrs Livingstone . . . bye.'

CHAPTER FIVE

'No I'm not. I'm *not* Joyce Ingham. What's *this* place, there was nothing here a minute ago.'

'It's all right, Joyce.' The woman holds up her hands, a calming gesture. 'You're upset, I understand. Lots of our pupils are upset when they first come to us.' She smiles. 'After all, it's very different from your old school, isn't it? Classrooms without walls, children working in coats and caps. Very strange, but you'll be surprised how quickly you'll get used to it.'

'Classrooms . . . ?'

I glance towards the nearest building and it's true: the place is just a floor and a roof supported

15

on wooden pillars, though it does appear to have one wall. And there are children, ten or twelve of them, muffled up, sitting at the sort of desks you see in historical movies. They've all got small, white faces, and every face is turned towards me.

The woman smiles again, slips a hand under my arm. 'Come, Joyce, we seem to be causing a distraction here. We'll sit in my study and have a little chat: just us two. And I'll have a look at that scratch on your cheek.' She starts steering me to a concrete path.

I jerk my arm away and shout, 'Where am I – where's Pip?'

'Did Pip bring you, dear? Is she your big sister?'

'Nobody *brought* me, I don't know how I got here. What *is* this place?'

The woman smiles, patiently. 'I'm sure you know where you are, Joyce. You're at Cold Tarn Open Air School. You've not been very well and you're here for the sake of your health, like all our pupils. Come along now.' She's taken my arm again.

'There's nothing wrong with my health,' I sob,

breaking free again. 'I'm off home.' I have a sudden thought and look at her. 'Is it a movie set: something for TV?'

She shakes her head. 'I've not the faintest idea what you're talking about, Joyce. I know you're upset: I understand that, but the doctors think you'll benefit from a year or two with us, and who are we to argue with them, eh? Here you are, and you might as well make up your mind to be sensible and try to fit in, because the sooner you do that, the sooner you'll be well enough to go home.'

'I'm *not* Joyce, I'm Charlie Livingstone and I'm not staying here.' I turn, set off running towards the woods, thinking, *Who are these characters? There's no school up here, they're kidnappers or something. Where the heck's Pip?* 'Piiiiiiiiip!'

I don't reach the woods. What happens is, a guy runs out of one of the classrooms and gets between me and the trees. I skid to a halt on the wet grass. He looks fit, I know I won't outrun him. Might as well save my strength. He slows to a walk when he sees I've given up, approaches grinning.

'Hello, Joyce, my name's Mr Newberry, I'm

the science teacher here. Funny old place, isn't it? Shall we join Miss Carrington? I happen to know she's got some chocolate biscuits in her cupboard.'

CHAPTER SIX

'Afternoon. My name's Detective Constable Stables. Are you Philippa Davis?'

'Yes.'

'And you say your friend's gone missing – Charlotte Livingstone?'

'Yes. She was here one minute, then gone.'

'Where was she, exactly, when you last saw her? Can you show me?'

'Yes, she was over there, by that bush.'

'Hmm. And then you looked away, for how long, would you say?'

'Oh – ten seconds. Something like that.'

'And when you looked again she wasn't

there. Did you *hear* anything: a cry or a gasp?'

'No.'

'Nothing at all?'

'Nothing.'

'I see. Was there anybody about, besides the two of you?'

'We didn't see anybody. People only come when there's ice on the tarn.'

'Mmm. *You* came, though. Why?'

'We like to walk, Charlie and me. Talking and that. We don't like crowds, so we come to the woods.'

'And what made you come out here?'

'It was these: these concrete things. We've never noticed them before, they must've been hidden by weeds.'

'I see. So you haven't been to this particular spot before, eh?'

'Never.'

'And you didn't come across any – er – good hidey-holes, or anything like that?'

'This *isn't* a trick, or a joke. We wouldn't do that. Charlie vanished, I looked everywhere before I phoned her mum. Yelled her name, even called her moby. Listen, a car's coming, that'll be

Charlie's mum. We wouldn't make her drive right up here for a laugh, would we? Not to mention the police.'

'No, I don't believe you would. Something funny's happened here, and I won't rest till it's sorted.'

CHAPTER SEVEN

Carrington's so-called study is in a proper building: one with walls. It's upstairs. I walk up after her, with this Newberry character at my heels. It feels like I'm in a play. I suppose it's shock.

'Sit down, Joyce,' she says, nodding towards a wooden chair, and I do. It's got a threadbare padded seat. Newberry chucks himself into an armchair, crosses his legs and winks at me. The woman opens a tall cupboard, reaches up and takes down a round tin with somebody royal on the lid. She puts the tin on her desk, opens it and holds it out to me. 'Go on, dear, take one, it's off the ration.' This must be some sort of joke, because Newberry laughs.

I shake my head. 'No thanks, I'm not a chocolate fan.'

She shrugs and offers the tin to Newberry who says, 'Oh right: *I*'ll have yours then, Joyce,' and takes two. Carrington, clearly irritated, replaces the lid without taking a biscuit herself, walks round the desk and sits in the swivel chair.

'Now.' She slides a sheaf of papers towards herself, riffles through them and looks at me. 'You were in Standard One at Crown Street Secondary School for Girls, Joyce: is that correct?'

I shake my head. 'I've never heard of it. I'm in Year Two at Blair Comp and my name's Charlotte Livingstone. I've never heard of this place and I'm scared, I don't understand what's happening.'

Carrington glances at Newberry, sighs and nods. 'You were at Crown Street, dear, and your name is Joyce Ingham. You're deeply upset and very unhappy, and we're accustomed to that here at Cold Tarn. We understand just how you're feeling, don't we, Mr Newberry?'

'Yes indeed, Headmistress.'

'It probably hasn't helped that your parents saw fit to let you find your own way here, after putting you into those – ah – somewhat bizarre clothes. Still, we know Joyce will be feeling heaps better in a day or two, don't we, Mr Newberry?'

'We do, Headmistress. Years of experience have taught us that.'

'They have, Mr Newberry.' She smiles at me. 'I'll tell you what I'm going to do, Joyce. We have a girl at this school who was every bit as upset as you are when she arrived two years ago. You know exactly who I'm talking about, don't you, Mr Newberry?'

'I believe so, Headmistress: Cissy Murgatroyd.'

The woman nods. 'Cissy Murgatroyd. Distraught, Cissy was, the day she came to us.'

'And for some days after,' adds Newberry.

'Just so. And now – what a transformation! From a poor, weedy little soul who wouldn't say boo to a goose, to the proud, strapping, confident girl who strides about this place with her head held high and her mind on loftier matters.' She stands up. 'I'm going to put you under Cissy's capable wing, Joyce. She's initiated many a new girl, even a boy or two.' She beams. 'Three days in Cissy's tender care, Joyce, and you'll wonder why you were ever upset. Eh, Mr Newberry?'

'Indubitably, Headmistress.'

CHAPTER EIGHT

'D.C. Stables, madam. Your daughter hasn't made her way home, I suppose?'

'I wouldn't be here if she had. Have you found anything?'

'I'm afraid not, but try not to worry at this stage. As I was saying to young Philippa here, we'll have it sorted in no time.'

'How can you say that, Officer, when you don't know? Where was she, Pip, just before you missed her?'

'Right here, Mrs Livingstone, where we're standing. We've looked for holes and stuff, and there's nothing. It's like Charlie vanished into thin air.'

'Yes, well, we *all* know that's impossible. There's a rational explanation, so let's find it.'

She turns to D.C. Stables who says, 'I'm going to call in, get some uniforms up here. We need to make a thorough search before it starts to get dark.'

CHAPTER NINE

Cissy Murgatroyd's waiting in the corridor. She sticks out a hand.

'I'm Cissy, and *I* blubbered too. Where'd you get those slacks, Joyce, and that peculiar coat?' She's big, with a broad, freckly face and frizzy ginger hair to match. We shake hands, it still feels like a play.

'It's not peculiar,' I snap. 'It's a hoodie. And I'm *not* Joyce, I'm Charlie.'

'Charlie's a boy's name.'

'Short for Charlotte, after Charlotte Brontë. My parents're fans.'

'They're *what*?'

'Fans. Brontë fans. They christened my little brother Acton.'

'Crumbs.'

'And the dog's Keeper, like *their* dog.'

'Goodness. And where do they live, your family?'

'Beagle Avenue, on the Hunter's Park estate. Number four.'

'Don't know it, is it far from here?'

'No, it's through the woods and down the hill. Can't miss it.'

'Hmm, wonder why I've not noticed it? Never mind: the Head said to show you round, so we'd best get weaving.'

I shake my head. 'No.'

'What d'you mean, *no*? We don't say no to an instruction from the Head.'

'I do. She's not *my* Head. Listen.' I look her in the eye. 'I don't know how I got here, or why everybody thinks I'm this Joyce Ingham, but I'm seriously brassed off with it. I'm phoning my friend, and we're off home.'

Cissy smiles, she's a face like a town clock. 'The telephone's in Miss Carrington's study, d'you think she'll let you use it?'

I fish in my pocket, pull out my moby, wave it at her. 'I've got my own, dummy.'

I thumb in Pip's number and select. Cissy Murgatroyd gazes at the instrument. I press it to my ear but nothing's happening. I look at the screen. 'No signal,' I snarl. 'I don't flipping believe it.'

'What *is* that thing?' goes Cissy. 'It's not a telephone, there's no wire.'

'It's a moby: don't tell me you've never seen . . .'

My voice stalls. There's something my brain's been trying to ignore because it's impossible. It dawned the moment I saw those antique desks, those gaunt, pasty faces, and it was boosted by Carrington's joke about the ration. I swallow hard, but my words still come out as a croak. 'What *year* is this?'

Cissy leers at me. 'It's nineteen fifty-two. Don't say you're going to claim you've been sent a year early, you were meant to come next year?'

I hardly hear her. There's a noise in my skull like the sea, and my heart's pounding my ribs. I slump against the wall to keep from falling down.

Cissy bends close, peering into my face. 'I say,

30

Joyce, are you all right? You've gone really pale.'

I look at her. 'N . . . Nineteen fifty-two?'

'Yes, of course.'

I stare at her. 'Can't be, it's impossible. It's a hoax, right? That TV show – what's it called – with hidden cameras?'

Cissy shakes her frizzy head. 'It's nineteen fifty-two, Joyce: the fourth of February to be exact. Look.' She lays an arm across my shoulders. 'I think I'd better take you back to the Head's study.'

I shrug to free my arm. 'No, listen, I need to be where she found me, the exact spot. You see, there's got to be a way back.'

CHAPTER TEN

We start back along the corridor, slowly, without speaking. Cissy Murgatroyd senses there's more to my behaviour than mere resentment, though she's no idea of the truth. If it *is* the truth. I can hardly believe it myself.

I mean, come on. Timeslips happen in books and movies, not real life. A part of me's clinging to the TV explanation, because it's less scary. I give it one more go.

'Are you an actress, Cissy?'

She snorts. 'Oh yes, I'm a Hollywood star with frizzy hair and freckles. Boys faint with desire at the sight of me.'

32

My heart slumps. 'So it's not TV then?'

Cissy shakes her head. 'They'll think you're a loony if you go on like this.'

'I'm not a loony. Look, I'll show you where I was when . . .' I try to pull her towards the stairs, but she resists.

'No, Joyce: I think the Head should hear what you've been saying to me. New girls often get upset, but—'

She's steering me towards the study door. I'm scared, hardly know what I'm doing. I lash out at her, break free and dash down the stairs.

CHAPTER ELEVEN

'Geoff, is that you? Where are you?'

'I've just left Sainsbury's car park, Sue: is something wrong?'

'Yes, it's Charlie, she's missing.'

'Missing? How can she be . . . ?'

'I don't know. She was with Philippa Davis, up by the tarn.'

'And?'

'Philippa phoned me, said she'd vanished.'

'How long ago was this?'

'Two hours, two and a half. The police're here now, searching.'

'You're up there *yourself*?'

'Of course I am, I'm frantic. They keep saying don't worry, but that's silly, isn't it? They're talking about dragging the tarn. I need you with me, Geoff.'

'Of course you do. I'll be fifteen minutes, tops. And Sue?'

'What?'

'Don't . . . forget it, I was about to say something silly. I'm on my way.'

CHAPTER TWELVE

I burst through the door and turn left, pelting round the end of the building. I'm looking across a wide lawn, cut here and there with neat oblong flower beds, though nothing is growing in them. Beyond I can see the classrooms. There are three and they're identical. I don't know which I need.

They'll be after me, there's no time to think.

I run across the soft lawn, heading for the last classroom: the one Newberry ran out of. I'm looking for the stepping stones, but I can't see them. I need time but I won't get it. A glance behind shows Newberry hot on my heels. Two

Biscuits, I've christened him. I'm not scared of him, but my situation terrifies me.

Think about it. I can head for the woods, and I might even make it, but they're not the woods of my *time*. These are the woods of half a century ago: more than twenty years before my parents were born. Hunter's Park isn't built yet: no wonder Cissy Murgatroyd's never heard of it. There's no Beagle Avenue, no number four. *There's no Charlotte Livingstone*. Here in the fifties I'm better off as Joyce Ingham: at least she exists.

So I stop running. I'm on a driveway that passes close to the classrooms. Beyond it is more lawn, dotted with leafless trees, and beyond that the woods. Behind me, panting a bit, comes Two Biscuits Newberry. *Act cool*, I tell myself, *wait for a better chance*.

'Now, Joyce, that wasn't very nice, was it: punching poor Cissy who was trying her best to be kind?'

'I'm sorry, Mr Newberry, I panicked: didn't know what I was doing.'

'I should hope you *are* sorry, young lady. Come: we'll make our way back and you can

37

apologize to her, and to Miss Carrington. Nobody here wishes you harm, Joyce.'

'No, Mr Newberry.'

He takes my elbow and we walk back past his classroom. The kids stare as we go by, but they stay in their seats and there's no commotion. At Blair Comp, a teacherless class will always riot.

Maybe this is what happens when you o.d. on fresh air.

CHAPTER THIRTEEN

I'm in Miss Stafford's class. Cissy Murgatroyd isn't: she's in Mr Fraser's, but all the girls sleep in the one dormitory and we'll see each other at breaks. She must be *really* nice because she's like, 'Don't worry, Joyce, I'm here to look out for you,' even though there's a yellowish bruise under her right eye where my fist caught her.

She tells me a bit about Open Air Schools. They're for delicate children, which means kids with chest problems, weak hearts, asthma: stuff like that. Joyce – that's *me* of course – has been sent here because she can't shake off bronchitis. It seems pupils' health improves hugely after a few weeks doing maths with snow on the desk. The words *yeah* and *right* run through my mind, but I keep 'em to myself. The classrooms do have one wall, by the way, facing north. *Anyway*, I tell myself, *it's only till I find those stepping stones*. A little voice inside my skull's like, *yes, but what if it doesn't work, this thing with the stepping stones?* but I tune it out. Have to, or I'll go barmy.

Miss Stafford's tall for a woman, and bony, in thick woolly kit and clumpy shoes. She's kind though. Patient. When Miss Carrington's introduced me and left, some of the kids start sniggering at my clothes. Stafford zaps 'em with a look that'd make a wall blush, guides me to sit next to a lad with *strong silent type* written all over him.

'There, Joyce: you'll be all right next to Jack – won't she, Jack?'

'Yes, miss,' grunts Jack, but he shuffles away a bit.

The lesson's geography. A shiny map of the world covers most of the one wall. On a ledge below the map is a box of pins with large coloured heads. How it works is, the teacher calls out somebody's name and the name of a capital city, and the kid has to find the city on the map and stick a pin in it. A freezing wind keeps gusting through the room, it rattles the map. Each pupil has a blanket to wrap round her legs when sitting, and they all wear chunky brown sweaters. I'm the only one without, and my hoodie's not all that good a substitute. I wrap my arms round myself to keep from dying of hypothermia. Miss Stafford notices after a bit and says, 'I think you'd better find Nurse Chickwood and ask her to issue your uniform and blanket, Joyce. Go with her, Jack.'

Jack discards his blanket and stands up. I follow him out of the room and along a concrete path. It's too narrow to walk side-by-side. He hurries along without speaking and I trot at his heels.

'Where's Nurse Chickwood hang out?' I ask.

'There.' He nods towards the two-storey block that has the Head's study in it. It'd like to get him talking, but he strides along as though he just wants this to be over.

The path takes us to the door I crashed through after I hit Cissy. Here are the stairs, but instead of taking them Jack hangs a left and we walk through a long room that echoes and smells like swimming baths. Along one side is a line of shower cubicles, along the other a slatted wooden bench with a row of metal pegs above it. At the end is a white tiled wall with a door in it.

Jack knocks, cracks open the door and says, 'Please, miss, Miss Stafford's sent the new girl.' He jerks his head at the opening and I walk in.

Nurse Chickwood's good at guessing sizes, there's no trying on. I get sweater, skirt and a long wool coat. There are thick socks too, and strong shoes, as well as a beret and some fleecy vests and knickers. I wouldn't choose this stuff myself, but it's really snug.

When I leave the nurse's room, Jack's gone. I'm supposed to take my own stuff to the girls' dormitory, but I don't know where it is. I think maybe this is my chance to look for those stepping stones, but then an old guy comes round the corner pushing a wheelbarrow and I ask directions instead. I'm not ready yet to find out if my way back will work. He directs me through a gap between two classrooms and across the main driveway. There are two blocks, the girls' is on the left. I'm relieved to see the dormitories have walls on three sides, being open only to the south.

I go in. There's nobody about. Two lines of narrow beds, a tin wardrobe by each bed. I notice each wardrobe has a little frame with a name card in it. I find Cissy's: C. MURGATROYD, in green crayon. All I have to do now is look for one with no card.

There isn't one. I end up working my way up and down the rows till I find the card somebody's done for me. Well, not for me of course: for Joyce. J. INGHAM it says, in blue. The wardrobe's empty, I stow my hoodie and other stuff. I hear kids' voices. Across the way, in front of a classroom, some boys are working with forks and rakes on a patch of soil and I think, *In my world, those kids're old men or dead, and here I'm not born yet. Even Mum's not born. I'd be better off in the middle of Antarctica or the Amazon jungle: at least there'd be a direction I could start walking in: a step closer to Mum, two steps . . .*

My predicament overwhelms me, so that I cover my face with my hands and weep.

CHAPTER FOURTEEN

'Does that feel better, Joyce?' I've been ages, geography's over, the kids're standing behind their chairs doing arm and neck exercises.

'Yes thanks, miss.' Stafford means the clothes, not my weepy session, though that seems to have helped a bit as well.

'Splendid.' She smiles. 'We're stimulating our circulations. Go to your place and join in.' I do it, treating Jack to a glare for not waiting. He ignores me, rotating his shoulders.

The warm-up ends with foot-stomping. There's a yelp from one of the girls. The teacher stops us, calls a boy out to the front and shouts at him.

'That's the second time this week you've deliberately stamped on Kathleen's foot, Martin Kent. Go to Mr Newberry, tell him why I've sent you.' The boy slinks out looking glum. Miss Stafford turns to the injured girl. 'All right, Kathleen?'

Kathleen has her foot on her chair and the boot off. She nods. 'Think so, miss.'

'Good.' She smiles at us all. 'Warmer now, everybody?'

Everybody is.

We're chanting our multiplication tables when Martin Kent comes back. He's got his hands tucked in his armpits and has been crying, though he tries his best to pretend he hasn't. I've heard stories about the stuff they used to do if you were naughty at school, so I know he's had the cane. I start wondering if girls get it, and lean towards Jack.

'Do they cane girls?'

'One nine is nine,' goes Jack. 'Two nines are eighteen, three nines are . . . the slipper . . . twenty-seven, four nines are thirty-six . . .'

The slipper. Yes, I can picture that. Wonder who swings it? Get four years for it at Blair Comp,

45

whoever it is. Best behaviour from now on, Charlie.

We chant on, up to our twelve-times. Twelve twelves are a hundred and forty-four. Surely that's it, it's so boring. I sneak a peek at my watch, but I'm not quite sneaky enough. Jack leans across, frowns and hisses, 'What the heck's *that?*'

'Watch.' I know why he's asking, of course. Digital. No such thing, here in the fifties. Is *now* though, and what's more it works, unlike the moby.

'Let's have a dekko.' He's leaning too far across, Miss Stafford's bound to notice. *Go to Mr Newberry, Joyce: say you've come for the slipper.* No thanks. I extend my arm so he can see without leaning.

'That's not a watch,' he growls. 'There's no dial and no hands. What is it *really?*'

'It's a watch,' I insist. 'A *digital* watch. You won't have heard of it, because it hasn't been invented yet.'

'Huh?' He gives me a funny look. 'Green van'll come for you, girl, any minute.'

I frown at him. 'What does that mean? *What* green van, Jack?'

He tuts. 'The one that takes you off to the nuthouse, of course.'

'Nuthouse?'

'Asylum. Lunatic asylum. Where they put people who've got things that haven't been invented yet.' He shakes his head. 'And once you're in, nobody'll ever see you again. You or your digital watch.'

CHAPTER FIFTEEN

It's half-eleven by my digital watch, and by the teacher's analogue as well. To my surprise, this is bedtime. 'Where we going?' I whisper to Jack, as Miss Stafford leads us out of the classroom.

'Bed,' he grunts. 'Bed in the shed.'

There's a long shed south of the classrooms. I'd noticed it on my way to the dormitory but didn't know what it was for. Turns out it's the resting shed, where the kids go for a nap before lunch. They get an afternoon nap too, though I don't know this yet.

It's only got one wall of course: an end wall facing north. There are four rows of narrow canvas beds on folding wooden frames. We've brought our blankets, which is just as well because there's no other covering. There are no pillows either, though the beds are a fraction higher at the head than at the foot. I want to ask Jack why we get this nap, but the shed has two rows for girls and two for boys, so he's not near me.

There's a wooden armchair against the wall, with a woman in it. She tells us to take our shoes off and lie on our right side under the blanket. I pull my blanket right up over my head, partly because it's perishing cold, but also because I feel daft lying in the middle of all these strangers when I've only ever slept in my own room. I don't want to look at them, and I certainly don't want them looking at me. But I haven't been like that for more than two seconds when somebody hisses my name. Well, not *my* name.

'Joyce!'

'Huh: what?' I poke my head out. It's Cissy Murgatroyd, in the next bed. I forgot to say all the classes nap together: it's a big shed.

'We're not allowed to cover our faces.'

'Why?'

'In case we talk.'

'We can't *talk*?'

'Course not, we're here to sleep.'

'I don't sleep in the daytime, that's for vampires.'

'Rest, then.'

'I don't *need* rest, I've only been sitting down.'

'You're not strong, none of us is, that's why we're here.'

'It's not why I'm here, I'm fit as a butcher's dog. I'm here because of a timeslip.'

'You don't half talk some gibberish, Joyce. Be quiet now, or Miss Paramenter'll report you to the Head.'

'Who's Miss Paramenter?'

'Nurse Chickwood's assistant: she's sitting over there.'

I don't sleep. I hardly ever lie on my right side, and on stretched canvas it's excruciating. My body manages to lie still, but my mind's racing. How the heck did I get here, can I go back the same way, and what if I *can't*? How can somebody live before their parents are born? It's not possible. In 1952 I'm an impossibility, so I can't really *be* here. Which makes me . . . what? Not a ghost: they're from the past. Not a figment of somebody's imagination: I'm too solid for that, look at Cissy's eye.

A visitor from the future, yes, but not like in stories. I'm not a bit curious about this weird place I've landed in. I don't care about it, I'm not interested in finding anything out, in fact I hate it. All I want is to get out of it, the sooner the better. In a story I'd have a machine: a time-machine. All I'd have to do is get in, set the dial at 2007, punch a button and POW! Home in time for tea.

I wish. I wish. I wish . . .

CHAPTER SIXTEEN

In the end I *do* sleep, and when I'm waking up I get one of those ideas that seem absolutely brilliant at the time. You wonder why you didn't think of it before.

My watch. All I have to do is show the teacher my watch. There's nothing like it in 1952, so she'll be forced to believe me when I tell her I'm from the future. There's no other way I could have such an instrument, is there? And once she accepts that, she'll have to admit I'm not Joyce Ingham. I feel better already.

I stick my hand up while we're queuing

outside the dining room, which is part of the main building.

'What is it, Joyce?'

'Miss, can I show you my watch?'

'Your watch, Joyce? Why?' Some of the kids are sniggering.

'Miss, because it's digital.'

'What on earth does that mean?' She approaches, looking puzzled.

I stick out my wrist. 'Look, miss, it's got no hands: doesn't need them.'

Miss Stafford takes hold of my hand, peers at the watch. 'Hmmm. Twelve thirty-six. That's the time all right, but what a peculiar thing. Where did you get it, Joyce?'

'They're common where I live, miss.'

'Are they? And where might that be, dear?'

'Two thousand and seven.'

'That sounds like a telephone number, Joyce: I meant what *town* or *city*.'

I shake my head. 'No, miss, it's not my phone number, it's the year.'

'What on earth are you saying, child: that you live in the year two thousand and seven? Fifty-five years from now?'

53

'Yes, miss.'

'Don't be absurd.' She narrows her eyes. 'You mustn't take advantage, Joyce, just because you're new. We try always to be kind and patient with our pupils here at Cold Tarn, but that doesn't mean we're prepared to put up with a lot of nonsense. Now, cover that silly toy with your sleeve and wait quietly, like everybody else.'

So, not the solution to all my problems, then.

CHAPTER SEVENTEEN

I'm at Cissy's table for lunch. Ten kids to a table. The dining room has walls, thank goodness, but in case we get soft they have all the windows wide open. Cissy's server at our table. The grub's OK but boring: cheese pie, mashed spuds, peas and gravy. For pudding it's spotted dick and custard. I remember Grandma saying there were no such things as burgers, pizzas or curries in her young day, so I suppose the food here's as good as anywhere.

There are five boys at our table. One of them is Martin Kent. He's got over his caning: in fact he's obviously proud of it, displaying his bruised palms to his pals and describing his ordeal in unnecessary detail. He got one on each hand, which another boy tells him is nothing but a tester.

'I *know*,' says Kent defensively, 'but it don't half sting, the way old Newberry lays it on.'

I'm horrified, listening. It's barbaric. If teachers do this to delicate kids, what might they do to healthy ones? My feelings must be showing on my face, because a boy called Kenneth Trubshaw leers across at me.

'What's up, Joyce: didn't they *have* the cane at your old school?'

'Hey, p'raps they had a *digital* cane,' laughs Kent. 'One that don't need *hands*.'

Everybody falls about, even Cissy. I smile, have to admit it's a nice one. I shake my head.

'There was no cane, not even a digital one: they abolished it.'

'Ooooh!' goes Trubshaw. 'I'm putting in for a posting to your old school, minute the docs let me out of here.'

Heads nod, there's a chorus of *me too*.

I pull a face. 'Let me know when, and I'll tag along.' I say this in a jokey way, but inside I'm close to cracking. We're talking about a school that isn't built yet, its teachers unborn. The place I'm in is the one Pip and I were playing around in, yet it's a foreign land.

No, it's *worse*. You can phone home from a foreign land.

CHAPTER EIGHTEEN

Lessons all afternoon – with another nap after
lunch first – then end at four, supper's at six,
seven's bedtime. *Seven*, for goodness' sake. Your
only free time's from four to six, and there are four
ways you can use it. You can go to the recreation
hut and listen to something called *The Children's
Hour* on radio, if you can stand the excitement. You
can read a book. You can write a letter home. *Mr
and Mrs Livingstone, 4 Beagle Avenue, Hunter's
Park, Speeton. Please don't deliver till 2007*. Yeah,
right. Or you can go for a walk, as long as you don't
leave the grounds. I feel like being by myself for a
while, so I choose the walk.

It's dusk already, but I head for the woods. Under the first trees I come to a picket fence. I turn left and follow it, up towards the tarn. I expect it to bar the way to the tarn, but it doesn't. When I reach the top, there's just enough light to show it looping right round the water before snaking downhill round the back of the school.

I set off round the tarn, then notice somebody ahead of me. A boy, slashing at dry reeds with a stick. After a bit he stops to look at something in the water, and I catch up. It's Jack. He doesn't know I'm here, I could just go by. But I want to speak.

'Hi, Jack.'

He glances round. 'Oh, hello.'

'What've you found?'

He points, I look. 'Frogspawn, right.'

He grins, shakes his head. 'Newtspawn. I love how everything seems dead this time of year, then you find spawn or a green shoot and you know it's all starting up again. There's wonders all round if you know how to look.'

I get a shivery feeling when he says this, don't know why. I gaze at him and say, 'I want to tell you something, Jack, but you mustn't laugh.'

He shrugs. 'Why should I laugh?'

'I hope you won't. It's about a wonder, like the spawn, but even weirder.'

'You mean, like that watch?'

I smile. 'Much weirder, Jack.'

He shakes his head. 'Can't be, unless you're going to say you came in a flying saucer, from another planet.'

I shake my head. 'It isn't that, but it's just as bizarre.'

'Go on, I'm listening.'

'I . . . I'm scared you won't believe me.'

'I'll believe you till I have proof you're lying, Joyce.'

I don't know why, but I knew he would. 'Well, for a start I'm not Joyce, my name's Charlotte Livingstone.'

He shrugs. 'OK, Charlotte, that's not hard to believe, 'cause I'm not Jack.'

'You're *not*?' My heart kicks. 'You mean you got here like *I* did, through a . . . ?'

'No, what I mean is I was *found*, as a baby. Nobody knew who I was, so they called me Jack Lee and I'm stuck with it.' He grins. 'I might be *Lord* somebody for all I know.'

'Lee?' I feel a pang. 'My grandad's a Lee, he's in hospital. *Will be*, I suppose I mean. P'raps you're related.'

Jack shrugs. 'P'raps. What else have you got to tell me?'

I shake my head. 'My name's the easy bit, Jack. It's what's *happened* to me that's weird.'

'And what's that?'

I take a deep breath. If he cracks out laughing, I'll die. I'm a squillion trillion miles from home and I need a friend.

'It seems I've travelled through *time*, not space.'

He nods, without the flicker of a smirk. '*Back* through time, I suppose?'

'Yes.'

He nods again. 'It'd *have* to be back, on account of the watch.'

I look at him. 'You mean you *believe* me, Jack?'

'Certainly, until there's a better explanation.' He looks at me. 'Did you bring any *other* marvellous inventions with you?'

I fish out my moby, hand it to him. 'It's a phone, works without a wire.'

'Like a radio?'

I nod. 'Sort of, but it won't work here. My mum'll be trying—' I fill up, cover my face with my hands.

He waits, then touches my hair with his fingertips. 'I . . . haven't got a mum, but I know about them.'

They're so hesitant, these words of his: so obviously heartfelt, that I laugh as I cry. 'It's OK, Jack,' I croak. 'I'll be fine, now that somebody believes me.' I lower my hands. 'You *do* believe me, don't you?'

He nods gravely. 'Course I do, Charlotte. Come on: we better be getting back.'

CHAPTER NINETEEN

'What time do you call this?'

It's Newberry, lurking in the shadows by the dining room. He doesn't look happy. Jack hasn't got a watch: most of the kids haven't.

'Dunno, sir,' he mumbles. 'We were talking.'

I look at my watch. 'It's ten past six, sir.'

He nods. 'Precisely, Joyce Ingham.' He looks at Jack. 'And what time's supper, Jack?'

'Six o'clock, sir.'

Newberry nods. 'Six o'clock. Not content with being ten minutes late yourself, you lead a new pupil astray by causing her to be late also.'

'Oh no, sir.' The words are out before I can

stop them. 'It's my fault. I was upset, saw Jack by the tarn and started laying my problems on him. He just listened, couldn't get away.'

'Hmm.' He cocks an eyebrow at Jack. 'That how it was, Jack?'

Jack nods. 'Pretty much, sir.'

'All right, Jack, go get your meal.' He turns to me. 'You know, Joyce, the Head put you under Cissy Murgatroyd's wing this morning: you should have gone to Cissy with your troubles. We're not fuddy-duddies here at Cold Tarn, but we don't encourage our girls and boys to pair off for midnight rambles.'

'It's hardly *midnight*.' I don't mean to say this either, but he's such a wuss.

'Don't be impertinent,' he snaps. 'You were out after dark with a boy. What d'you suppose your mother would say if she knew?'

'She . . . it's different, sir, where I live. Kids are out till late, my mum'd be cool.'

'Where *you* live? Must be a bizarre neighbourhood.' He shakes his head. 'P'raps that's why you were sent to us. Anyway, your mother's not the only one who's cool: I'm half-frozen. In you go to supper now, and think yourself lucky. If this wasn't your first day, it'd be the slipper for you in the morning.'

Midnight. Slipper. It'll be my fairy godmother next.

CHAPTER TWENTY

'What happened to *you*, new girl?' This from Kathleen Rayner in the next bed. I'm half-undressed, hurrying because Nurse Chickwood's standing in the doorway of the little room she sleeps in, watching us. Kathleen's whispered without moving her lips. I answer in the same way.

'Nothing, me and Jack were talking, forgot the time.' I'm putting on the pyjamas Chickwood gave me this morning. They're thick and scratchy.

'Flogging offence, late for supper.'

'Flogging?'

'Yes, the dreaded slipper,' the girl on my other side chips in, I don't know her name. 'Miss Carrington does it, she's a right arm like a navvy. Your bum's tender for a week.'

I shake my head, getting into bed. 'I'm not getting it, Mr Newberry let me off.'

'Hoo, you were lucky then. Great believer in flogging, old Newberry, like Captain Bligh.'

The nurse stands with folded arms till we're all lying down, then turns away and closes her door.

'I call him Two Biscuits,' I say, to neither girl in particular. Kathleen asks why, and I tell her what happened in Carrington's study. I'm talking to Kathleen, but others are listening and there are giggles when I describe the look on the Head's face.

'She'd be absolutely *livid*,' chuckles another girl I don't know. 'Her brother gets those biscuits for her, he's boss of the firm that makes 'em. He can't get many and she hoards them like the crown jewels. Wonder she didn't give old Newberry the slipper.' She smiles, sleepily. 'Good nickname though, Two Biscuits.'

The lights go out, we're left in total darkness except for a strip of yellow under Chickwood's door. My companions are well trained: the talking ceases at once, and if it were not for the hacking coughs of girls with bad chests, there'd be silence.

No joke, coughing. Listening to it, I mean. I'm shattered, even though I've been to bed twice already, but sleep's impossible. I know they can't help it, but it's maddening the way the coughers seem to take it in turns to punctuate the darkness with their monotonous noise, leaving no gap of silence I can escape through into sleep. I want to scream at them to control themselves, drink some water instead of just lying there, barking.

It sounds pathetic but I start to cry. Not out loud: I mustn't let anybody hear me, but I can't not cry. I bury my face in the pillow that smells of camphor and cry for my mum. I know: twelve years old and crying for my mum, but nobody's ever been in this horrible predicament except in stories. I'm scared, and I'm really, really sorry for myself, and crying for my mum's nothing compared to what I easily *could* do, which is lie on the floor and scream and scream and scream. I think I might end up doing that anyway, but for now two things stop me. One, I'd probably be even worse off in the nuthouse. And two, Jack believes me.

Jack believes me.

CHAPTER TWENTY-ONE

'Charlie, is that you?'

'Mrs Livingstone?'

'Oh . . . it's Philippa, isn't it? I thought, I was hoping—'

'I'm sorry, Mrs Livingstone, I shouldn't have called. My mum told me not to, only I wondered if they'd found . . . if Charlie's turned up yet?'

'No, Philippa, she hasn't, and we're needing to keep this line open in case she tries to get in touch.'

'Yes, of course. I'll hang up straight away. Please could you give me a call if . . . when she shows up?'

'I will, Philippa.'

'Th-thanks. I'm off back to the woods this morning to look for her. Bye.'

'Goodbye, Philippa.'

What if she tried to call while I was on the line?

CHAPTER TWENTY-TWO

It's as cold as yesterday if not colder, but I've got my blanket now, and my jumper. Miss Stafford's teaching about Kings and Queens of England. We haven't covered that at Blair Comp: all I know is when Elizabeth the Second became Queen, and I only know *that* because my Grandma Lee won a prize at school for a poem she wrote when the old King died. It was a certificate, and it's on her bedroom wall. What I've only *just* realized is that King George died on 6 February, 1952: that's *tomorrow*.

I can't decide whether to mention it. Will it help prove my story if I do, or will they just think

I made a lucky guess? I mean, the King must be poorly if he's about to die. Nobody'd need a crystal ball. I nudge Jack.

'What?'

'Is the King poorly?'

'What, Henry the Seventh?' Miss Stafford's reached Henry the Seventh.

'No, dummy, King George the Sixth: the one you've got now.'

Jack whispers out of the corner of his mouth. 'Was, but they done an operation: said so on the wireless. Why?'

'He dies tomorrow.'

'How the heck do *you* know?'

'You *know* how I know. Or was I wasting my time last night?'

'Are you talking while I'm speaking, Joyce Ingham?' The teacher glares at me.

'No, miss,' I lie.

'Then who did King Henry the Seventh hang in fourteen ninety-nine? I've just told you.'

'Dunno, miss.'

'No, because you weren't paying attention. It was Perkin Warbeck: who was it?'

'Perkin Warbeck, miss. Miss?'

Miss Stafford sighs. 'What *is* it, Joyce?'

'The King, miss. He'll die tomorrow.'

'What are you talking about, girl? *Which* King?'

'This one, miss. King George.'

She frowns. 'Our King underwent an operation, Joyce, which his doctors say was successful: they speak of a full recovery.' She smiles sarcastically. 'But perhaps you know better than they do. Do you?'

I know that I *ought* to do. I ought to look at the floor and murmur, 'No, miss: sorry, miss.' That way I might just avoid more trouble than I'm in already, if that's possible. But something drives me to persist in the truth. The dangerous truth.

'Yes, miss, I do. And Princess Elizabeth's somewhere in Africa, miss, watching wildlife, and they tell her her father's died and she's Queen.'

Dead silence, except for the wind in the rafters. Everybody's looking at me.

After what feels like ages, Miss Stafford speaks. 'I think you'd better go and tell Miss Carrington your news, Joyce,' she says. 'She's got the perfect cure for girls who tell wicked stories.'

CHAPTER TWENTY-THREE

I don't want to tell Miss Carrington. Why should I? I'm not a pupil here, I'm not Joyce Ingham, she's no right to punish me. In fact in my world, my *time*, she's dead.

When I was younger I watched a video of *Alice in Wonderland*. This girl, Alice, goes down a rabbit hole into a fantasy world where animals talk and all sorts of weird stuff happens. It's like a dream. And she meets this queen, the Queen of Hearts, who keeps shouting *off with her head*, meaning Alice's head, only it doesn't happen because the queen's really nothing but a playing-card, the Queen of Hearts. And the thing is, you get the feeling Alice knows this all along, even though people don't usually know it's only a dream till they wake up.

What I'm saying is, I'm in what they call an Alice in Wonderland situation, dawdling up a concrete path that doesn't exist any more, to confront somebody who died before I was born. The whole thing's like a dream, and Carrington's only powerful inside it. If I could just wake up she'd be gone – *pouf!* – like that.

'Come in.' She's solid enough, sitting behind her desk. Especially that right arm.

'Joyce.' She smiles and looks surprised at the same time. 'The uniform's nice on you: are you beginning to feel more settled, dear?'

'Not really, miss, I feel like Alice in Wonderland.' I expect the smile to vanish, like the Cheshire Cat, but it doesn't.

'Still feeling as if you've fallen down a rabbit hole, eh? Never mind dear, it'll pass. What can I do for you?'

'Miss Stafford sent me, miss, to tell you about the King.'

'The King?' She looks surprised again. 'What about the King, Joyce?' She smiles. 'Not coming to visit our school, is he?'

'No, miss, he's going to die.'

'Die?' That's wiped the smile off. 'W-what d'you mean, dear? Who *told* you the King's going to die?'

'Nobody told me, miss. I know because I'm from the future. He dies tomorrow, at Sandringham.'

'Well, now.' She picks up a paper clip and fiddles with it, straightening it out. It's obvious she doesn't know what to say to me: if she's thinking *off with her head*, it doesn't show. I look past her, out of the window. Sleet hisses against the pane. After a bit she looks up.

'I hoped we were over all this silliness, Joyce: *I'm from the future*. Cissy *told* me you asked her what year this was, as if you'd stepped out of a time-machine or something. Goodness *knows* what put it into your head: H. G. Wells perhaps. Anyway it's got to stop, or people will start to question your sanity.' She drops the ruined clip in her waste paper basket, rubs her hands together and looks me in the eye. 'As for the ridiculous tale of yours concerning the King, you will come to me at this time tomorrow and I will help you

write a letter of apology to Miss Stafford, since
His Majesty will certainly be alive and well. Have
I made myself quite clear, Joyce?'

'Yes, miss.'

CHAPTER TWENTY-FOUR

Tuesday afternoon's basket weaving and we have it outside. Outside as in *under the sky*, not even in the windy classroom. This old guy, Mr Case, comes to teach it. The expression *basket case* occurs to me of course, but when I try it out on Jack there's no reaction. I don't think they have it in '52.

We carry our chairs out and arrange them in a half-circle under some trees. Jack says they're fruit trees, but you can't tell in February. 'I thought they were *lavver-trees*,' I quip, and this time he laughs.

It's not as easy as it looks, weaving baskets,

but it breaks up the school day a bit, which is why we have it. They reckon delicate kids can't concentrate on academic stuff all day, even with naps. Personally, I'd much prefer maths in a room with walls and central heating, but then I'm not delicate.

One good thing about being outside with Mr Case is, you're allowed to talk. Softly. Jack takes the opportunity to probe me about some stuff I told him last night.

'So these satellites,' he murmurs, 'they send 'em up on rockets, do they?'

'Yes. The Russians do it first, five years from now.'

'That'll be nineteen fifty-seven.'

'That's right. Sputnik One. We did it in history.'

'And it made those whats it . . . cell phones work?'

I shake my head. 'Not back then. Sputnik One didn't do anything except transmit a beep: it was an experiment.'

'Oh.' He sounds disappointed.

'Sputnik Two had a dog in it,' I offer.

'What for?'

I shrug. 'Dunno. To see what'd happen to a living creature in space, I suppose. Laika was its name.'

'And what *did* happen?'

'It died.' I gave him a sideways glance. 'You do believe me about all this stuff, don't you, Jack?'

He shrugs, grins. 'Put it this way: if you're making it up you should be writing for *Amazing Science Fiction*. You'd be rich and famous.'

'Amazing . . . ?'

'Magazine I read sometimes. Good writers, but not a patch on your stuff.'

'Course not: my stuff's true.'

He grins. 'You could send it in anyway, they wouldn't know.'

I shake my head. 'I might if I was staying here, Jack, but I'm not.' I nod towards the classrooms. 'Somewhere over there is a path from now to two thousand and seven. It's invisible, but I was on it yesterday and I'll be on it again the minute I find it. I'm interested in that, not stories.'

'What a *title* though,' murmurs Jack. '*The Path*

to Two Thousand and Seven. Win an award, that would: a Nebula.'

I nod. '*You* write it, Jack, after I've gone.' A thought occurs to me; I look at him. 'Hey: I wonder if you *did*?'

CHAPTER TWENTY-FIVE

My so-called basket's a mess. All I've got when old Case calls time is the base I had to start with, and a loose tangle of withes pointing every which way. 'Cuckoo's nest,' he growls when I hand it in, but he's smiling. The teachers seem to have more patience than ours at Blair Comp.

We're carrying our chairs back to the class-room when Jack says, 'What about flying saucers, Charlie?' He's taken to calling me Charlie where nobody can hear.

I glance at him. 'What about them?'

'Well, with all those rockets and satellites and stuff, you're bound to get close to flying saucers, so what *are* they: is somebody in 'em?'

I smile, shake my head. 'There's no such thing, Jack. People report them, but there's always a boring explanation. Stephen Hawking says if we were being watched we'd know, and we wouldn't like it.'

'Who's Stephen Hawking?'

'He's a brilliant scientist. *Will* be, I suppose I mean. He's a boy at the moment.'

We reach the classroom. Jack plonks down his chair. 'So there's no *two little men*?'

'Huh?'

'Aw, you know.' He starts singing:

> '*Two little men in a flying saucer*
> *Flew round the Earth one day*
> *Once they saw the sight of it*
> *They were all afright of it*
> *And quickly flew away.*'

He's better at baskets than singing. I shake my head. 'Don't give up the day job, Jack.'

'What?'

'Just a saying we have. And no, there's no little men: sorry.'

Miss Stafford reads us a chapter from *Treasure Island*, then it's our free time. Jack's still bursting with questions, but we daren't go off like yesterday. We borrow chairs and sit in the lee of the main building, which has the dining room in it. We chat for a while but I'm restless, torn between wanting to keep Jack's friendship and needing to find that path. I'm worried about what'll happen when I turn out to be right about the King. If there's one thing I don't need on top of everything else, it's to be thought of as some sort of witch, so now would be a handy time to disappear.

'Jack?'

'What?'

'I . . . want a shot at getting back home.'

'Now?'

'Yeah, now. Help me?'

'Course. What do we do?'

'It's over by the classrooms, I'm not sure where exactly. Is there a path, like stepping stones?'

'I never seen one.'

'Well, there is in two thousand and seven, and

it's got something to do with it. Let's look before it's too dark.'

We return blankets and chairs to the class-room and pace the short grass, looking at the ground. We've not been at it five minutes when Cissy Murgatroyd shows up.

'What's up, Joyce, lost something?'

I don't want her here. I shake my head. 'No. Well yes, but not like you mean. We're looking for the way back.'

'Ah, the way *back*.' She nods towards Jack. 'You picked the right chum, then. Jack's our resident loony, you know: forever wandering off by himself, communing with nature. Runs away from time to time too.' She smiles. 'I'd like to help, but Miss Carrington's considering making me Head Girl, and you can't be Head Girl and a resident loony at the same time: it's against the rules.' She smiles. 'If you're late for supper, I'll tell Mr Newberry you found the way back, shall I?'

CHAPTER TWENTY-SIX

We don't find it and I'm gutted, even though I warned myself in advance not to hang by my feet: nothing's ever that easy.

Supper's shepherd's pie. Cissy serves my dollop with a smile. 'Didn't find it then, eh, Joyce?'

'Find what?' goes Martin Kent.

'I'm talking to the organ-grinder,' snaps Cissy, 'not the monkey.'

Martin blushes, changes the subject. 'She says the King's going to die.'

Cissy nods. 'We're *all* going to die, Martin: this shepherd's pie could do it.'

'No, she reckons he'll die *tonight*. Miss Stafford sent her to tell the Head.'

'Oooh!' hoots Trubshaw, who isn't in my class. 'So you've had the slipper already: show us your bum.'

'We'll have none of that sort of talk at *my* table,' warns Cissy, 'unless you fancy telling Miss Carrington what you just asked Joyce to do.'

'No fear,' mumbles Trubshaw.

'Then keep it buttoned.' She turns to me. 'Where'd you get *that* from then, Joyce: about the King?'

'From my gran: she's got a certificate.'

'Yeah,' mocks Martin, 'and you'll have a certificate and all, when they certify you.'

'Shut up, Martin,' snarls Cissy. 'And what did the Head say?'

I shrug, wishing I'd found the stepping stones tonight. 'If I'm wrong, I have to go to her tomorrow and write a letter of apology. But I'm not wrong.'

'No,' says Cissy gently: she's obviously decided I'm barmy. 'Of course you're not, Joyce. Eat your supper.'

* * *

It's a relief to be in bed, in the dark. At least nobody's mocking me, asking questions. There's no sleep, though. Wouldn't be anyway probably, because of the coughing, but it's this King business. I definitely shouldn't have said anything: I was stupid. It'd be bad enough, lying here knowing the poor guy's last hours're ticking away, without having to worry about what'll happen to me in the morning, when everybody finds out I was right. If only Jack and I had found those stepping stones.

There's a little voice in my head, it won't go away. *There are no stepping stones*, it whispers, *so maybe there's no way back. What if you have to stay here while your mum and dad get born down in Speeton; live out your life knowing everything that's going to happen before it does: fashion, bands, computers. News that's history, mobiles when you're too old to want them.*

It's no use, I can't face it. I'll lose my mind, they'll send a green van, I'll be certified, just like Martin said. I must go now, before I flip.

No use waiting till everyone's settled, it doesn't happen here. Not with all the bad chests. Just have to hope whoever spots me thinks I'm off for a wee: toilets're down one end of the dorm. I slip out of bed, grab my jumper, creep along the row.

Outside it's windy but dry. Sky full of stars. I pull the jumper over my pyjamas, tiptoe barefoot across the path and hurry over the icy grass to where the classrooms lie, dark and silent.

At first I search methodically, pacing back and forth, scanning the ground, and it's soon obvious, even in the dark, that there's no line of stones. I suppose deep down I expected that: if there were stones, surely Jack would know.

So I start to get desperate. Somebody'll have seen me up, they'll think I'm a long time at the toilet. Sooner or later they'll knock on Nurse Chickwood's door, because not every delicate kid is cut out for the open air life. They get runaways.

I quicken my pace, making little dashes through the spaces between classrooms. I curse myself for not having taken more notice of my surroundings when the slip happened. If I could remember exactly where, it'd be dead easy. I'm talking to myself now, gibbering, making little leaps because that's what I was doing when . . .

I can't keep it up of course. Leaping, sprinting,

gibbering. It's amazing nobody comes but they don't, so I caper in the moonlight in my pyjamas till I wear myself out and fall down, weeping.

The moon's almost set when I creep back to the dorm. I wonder if it's shining through the window of my room at home, laying a silver bar across my empty bed. I ought to cry at the thought, but I've left all my tears on the grass, where they'll be pips of ice by dawn.

CHAPTER TWENTY-SEVEN

'Children.' Carrington's come into the class-room, quietly. It's eleven o'clock, we're doing long division. My heart lurches. I've been on tenterhooks since I woke up this morning, bleary-eyed: waiting for whatever will happen. When breakfast passes without incident, and first period English, and morning break, I begin to hope I got it wrong. I won't mind writing that letter: it's being proved right I dread. I place my penholder in its groove, gaze at the Head.

'Children, I have sad news for you.' *Oh no:*

please . . . 'His Majesty the King died in his sleep early this morning.'

Gasps from the kids. Some turn to look at me. Miss Stafford pulls a little hanky out of her handbag and dabs her eyes. Carrington continues in a hushed voice. 'As a mark of respect, I am suspending all lessons for the remainder of the day. You are to gather with the other classes in the dining room, where we shall pray for His Majesty's soul. Move quietly please, in keeping with the situation.'

I wait for her to glance at me but she doesn't. She murmurs briefly to Miss Stafford, then leaves. We stand, fold our blankets and line up on the path. Jack passes close to whisper in my ear. 'They'll have to believe you now.'

Doesn't happen like that. I'm OK while we're in the dining room: nobody dares talk, so nobody's on my case. And I have to say Miss Carrington does a great job, considering she's cobbled the whole thing together at no notice. Well, she had notice from me, I suppose, but she didn't believe me so it doesn't count. Anyway, she manages to make it a really moving occasion without sliding into mush, which some people would. Credit where it's due.

When we're dismissed, we can read or walk in the grounds or play board games in the recreation hut. We mustn't play ball games or run, there's to be no noise. Apparently morning nap counts as a lesson: it's cancelled. I'm in the dorm getting my hoodie when Cissy Murgatroyd appears.

'The Head wants to see you in her study, Joyce,' she says. 'Right away.'

I traipse up the path. I'd hoped she'd choose to forget my Mystic Meg impression, but I guess it was a hope too far. I knock.

'Come. Ah, Joyce. Sit there, dear.' She nods to the chair I sat in before. I sit. 'Well.' She clasps her hands, gazes at me across the desk. 'It seems you were right, Joyce: I hope you take no pleasure in it.'

'I don't, miss. I wish I hadn't said anything.'

'It was a guess, of course: nothing more. In happier circumstances, one might call it a *lucky* guess.'

I could say, 'Yes, miss,' and escape with a telling-off, but I want to force her to believe the unbelievable. I don't know why really: it won't help me get home, but at least she might stop calling me Joyce. I shake my head.

'It wasn't a guess, miss. I knew it was going to happen.'

She snorts. 'You mean you have the gift of *prophecy*, Joyce?'

'No, it isn't prophecy, miss. I know because I'm from the year two thousand and seven. It's history.'

She sighs. 'You disappoint me, Joyce. I warned you yesterday that if you persist in this absurd nonsense, people will begin to question your sanity. Don't you see that what you are claiming is quite impossible?'

I shrug. 'It was impossible to know the King would die, but I did.'

'No, you did *not*, you made a guess.' She locks eyes with me. 'I'm giving you one last chance to abandon your preposterous pose as a girl lost in time, Joyce. If you do not, I will have no choice but to write to your parents and tell them I'm concerned about your mental state. Now: which is it to be?'

When I don't answer, she says, 'Cissy

Murgatroyd watched you capering barefoot in your pyjamas last night, Joyce. Capering and gibbering under the moon. What would *you* think, if you saw somebody doing that?'

'I'd think they were barmy, miss,' I murmur.

CHAPTER TWENTY-EIGHT

What I'm actually thinking is, *let her write to Joyce Ingham's wrinklies: they'll soon tell her I'm not their daughter.*

Miss Carrington nods, looks sad. 'Do you genuinely believe yourself to have travelled to Cold Tarn from the future, dear?' She doesn't want to write to anybody about me: she wants me to say no, but I can't, can I? If I do, Charlotte Livingstone disappears into limbo and becomes Joyce Ingham. And I'm *not* Joyce Ingham. In my time, Joyce Ingham's either an old, old woman, or dead.

Dead. My heart lurches as something occurs

to me. Something I should have thought of yesterday, or the day before: *where's the real Joyce Ingham?* I look at Carrington.

'Where is Joyce Ingham, miss? She might've been murdered. Why don't you phone her mum, check if she never set off?'

She ignores my suggestion and says, 'Since you obviously intend to stick to your story, Joyce, I have no option but to write that letter. And until such time as I have your parents' response, you will remain under Nurse Chickwood's care, in the Sick Room.'

Wonder why I can't keep my big mouth shut?

CHAPTER TWENTY-NINE

'Come along, Joyce.' Nurse Chickwood speaks softly, like I'm four. There's been a whispered conversation between her and the Head, who's probably told her I'm barking. As we head for the door Miss Carrington says, 'I hope you've thought about the distress this will cause your parents, Joyce. There needn't be a letter, if only you'll make your mind up to be sensible.' I don't respond.

The Sick Room's where I went for my school clothes. There's a desk, a few wooden chairs and two beds with scarlet blankets. 'Sit down, Joyce,' goes Chickwood. 'Now.' She smiles. 'Miss

Carrington and I both know that you are a very unhappy girl at the moment.' She shakes her head. 'It isn't your fault: you're ill, but we know a doctor who will make you well in a jiffy.' She moves to the desk, shuffles some papers around. 'Miss Carrington will write to him, and he'll send for you in due course.'

I look at her. 'Miss Carrington didn't mention a doctor. It's the loony-bin, isn't it? You want to put me in the loony-bin.'

'It's not ... we don't call it *that*, Joyce. It's a hospital: a psychiatric hospital. They make people well, just like any other hospital.'

I shake my head. 'Not me. They can't make me well 'cause I'm not ill, but they'll never let me out 'cause they won't believe me, even though I'm telling the truth.'

'What *is* the truth, Joyce?'

'That I'm Charlotte, not Joyce, and I belong in the year two thousand and seven.'

'Mmmm.' She nods. 'Yes, well you see, that's what your illness causes you to *believe*, Joyce. It's what we call a *delusion*: the doctor will make it go away and you'll be fine.'

I shake my head. 'It won't go away because it's

not a delusion, so they'll say I'm not cured. I'll be stuck there for ever.' I start to cry, can't help it.

'Hey.' Nurse Chickwood kneels, wraps her arms round me. 'It won't be like that at *all*, dear. Remember, Miss Carrington is writing to your parents. They'll be there when you get to the hospital. The doctor will talk to them, explain what—'

'No!' I'm shouting, shaking my head. 'Not my parents, they're not even born.' I stand up. 'Why am I here with you? Why can't I go to classes? *Tell* me.'

She puts her hands on my shoulders, presses gently till I sink onto the chair. 'I expect Miss Carrington's afraid you might run away,' she soothes. 'But I'm sure you're much too sensible to do that.'

Don't count on it, I think but don't say. *I'm barmy, remember.*

CHAPTER THIRTY

'Hello, Dad. How d'you feel?'

'Good as I ever will, Sue. Charlotte back yet?'

'No, Dad, she isn't. The police try to sound optimistic when they're with Geoff and me, but we're beginning to think . . .'

'How long's it been?'

'Three days. She's got a phone, she'd have called if she was . . . if she could.'

'Don't work everywhere though, do they? Mobiles.'

'No, Dad, but—'

'She'll be back, Sue, you'll see.'

'Yes, and she'll want to see you, so hurry up and get well, eh?'

'She's with me in the nick of time, Sue, you'll see.'

'Don't say *that*, Dad.'

'Huh? Oh, take no notice, sweetheart. It's the morphine, makes me ramble . . .'

CHAPTER THIRTY-ONE

It might not be too bad if Joyce's folks were coming *here*, but they're not. The way Carrington's fixed it, it's all going to happen at the loony-bin and I can't let it. I *can't*. It'll prove I'm not Joyce, but then I'm left with a true story that makes me sound insane. They'll throw away the key.

So I've got to escape, but *then* what? Could I make a life for myself here, in 1952? Kids do it all the time, don't they? I mean, they don't go back in *time*, but their whole family dies in a crash or something, or they get adopted by strangers in a foreign country and they have to start over, being somebody else. I don't want to think about having to do it, but anything's got to be better than being locked away.

Nurse Chickwood's in and out. Every time she leaves the room she locks the door. It's doing my head in. After about the sixth time I've had enough.

'Why d'you lock me in?' I ask. 'I'm not planning to run off, there's nowhere for me to go.'

'No dear, I know,' she says, 'but it's for your own good.'

'*How* is it for my own good?' I'm raising my voice, can't help it. 'I thought this was an open air school: how come open air's good for everybody else, but not me?'

She sighs, shakes her head. 'You say you won't run off, Joyce, but how do we know? You're not well: you might harm yourself and we're responsible.'

'So I'm locked away. What happens at night?'

'How d'you mean?'

I sigh. 'Do I sleep in the dorm?'

'No, no, you sleep here. Miss Paramenter will be with you.' She buzzes off again, doesn't want to talk.

When she comes back, she's got my lunch on a tray. Steak and kidney pudding, carrots, mashed potato and gravy. She puts the tray on her desk. 'You can eat here if you like, it'll be easier than on your lap.' She leaves, locking up same as always.

I've no appetite, poke at the food till it gets cold. At half one my jailer returns, makes me lie on the bed. It's afternoon nap, the kids're all in the resting shed. To my surprise, I wish I was with them.

I toss and turn. At least in here I don't have to lie on my right side all the time. I keep looking at my watch, so the hour goes slowly. At half two I get up. Chickwood's out, so I stand at the window. It opens, but two slender bars make it impossible to squeeze through. I breathe cold air. Some boys are raking a plot of earth. I recognize Jack and try to attract his attention, but the plot's too far away.

Chickwood comes back and slams the window, and I have to sit down with the book she's brought me. It's *Jane Eyre*, the one that features a mad woman. So thanks a bunch, Nurse: very sensitive of you. It's my mum's favourite novel as it happens: I'm named after its author, and there *wasn't* a *Joyce* Brontë.

One line's famous, it says: *Reader, I married him*. In this copy, some kid's crossed out *married* and put *throttled*. Well, you've got to have a laugh, haven't you?

CHAPTER THIRTY-TWO

Jack comes to the window when Chickwood's off getting my supper. It's twenty past five, nearly dark. I'm reading *Jane Eyre*, don't know he's there till he raps on the glass. I damn near jump out of my skin 'cause I'm on the bit about the mad woman in the attic.

I push up the window. 'Hi.'

'Hi yourself,' he says. 'What's happening: why are you in there, Charlie?'

I shake my head. 'They've decided I'm barmy, Jack: scared I'll run away. Carrington's writing to my folks: she means *Joyce*'s folks of course.'

He frowns and grins at the same time. 'Well,

108

isn't that OK? I mean, *they'll* soon tell her you're not their daughter.'

'No it's *not* OK, Jack, it's a green van situation.'

'How d'you mean?'

'She's calling some shrink at the loony-bin. That's where the Inghams're supposed to meet me, but I can't go there: they'd lock me up for life.'

Jack nods. 'Yes, I can see how they might.' He looks up at me. 'What d'you want me to do, Charlie?'

'You mean you'll help me?'

He nods. 'Course I will: *I* was the school nut till you got here, and us nuts've got to stick together.'

The bars stop me hugging him. I grin. 'Thanks, Jack, I mean it.' Then frown. 'Dunno what we can actually do, though.'

He stands back, fists on hips. 'Well, we can get you out of there for a kick-off.'

'Can we? Door's locked.'

He laughs. 'Door's locked, key's on a nail by the stairs.'

'How d'you know?'

'Always is.'

'OK, but then what?'

'Not sure yet.' He glances left and right. 'I better get cracking or Chickwood'll be back. Stand by.'

I put my hoodie on and hover near the door, my head spinning. *Is running away the best thing to do? Where can I go? And what about Jack? Runaway boys're caned if they're caught, and they're always caught in the end.*

And what if the nurse comes now? Or now? Or now?

I jump as a key rattles in the lock. Is it Chickwood, or Jack? I back off in case it's the nurse, but it opens and Jack sticks his head in. 'Come on, quick as you like.'

We stride past the showers. I haven't had one, and I don't suppose I will now. At the door, Jack stops me and peers out. 'All clear.' We turn right, running along the side of the block till we're outside Chickwood's room again. Jack creeps to her window and peeps over the sill. If she was to look out in the next few seconds, she'd see us pelting across the pathway and out over the lawn. 'OK.' She's not back. We run like the clappers, heading for the woods.

Under the trees we pause and look back. There are lights in the main block and the dormitories, the other buildings are dark. Nobody's following so we haven't been seen, but Chickwood'll raise the alarm the second she finds I've gone. We help each other over the fence and move into the middle of the woods before we stop for a breather.

'I don't know about this, Jack,' I pant. 'For one thing, I need to be near the spot we were looking for last night. There's nowhere for me here, in nineteen fifty-two, and what about you? Why should you make an outlaw of yourself, just to help me? Newberry'll half kill you if you're caught.'

Jack shrugs. 'I'm the school nut, remember? I've been half killed before, so don't worry. As for *you*, Charlie, you've got so many problems you can only tackle 'em one at a time. First up, they think you're Joyce Ingham, so let's prove you're not, eh?'

'Well yeah, but like *how*, without going near the loony-bin?'

'Easy: we go see the Inghams.'

'We don't know where they are, Jack.'

'*I* do.'

'How, for Pete's sake?'

'Ah.' He fishes in his trouser pocket, produces a scrunched-up scrap of paper, smooths it out. 'Here's the address, I copied it down. Look: a hundred and thirty-two Pearlman Street, Wolverstone.'

'*Wolverstone?* That's about six million miles away, Jack. Where'd you get it anyway?'

He grins. 'It was on the envelope that has Carrington's letter in it.'

'But how the heck did you get hold of it?'

'Easy. Outgoing mail's in a box under the stairs in the main block, ready for the postman to pick up in the morning.' He winks. 'I've been at Cold Tarn for ever, remember: I know where *everything* is.'

I shake my head. 'Not my stepping stones.'

Jack pulls a face. 'Because there aren't any, Charlie. So.' He smiles. 'That's where we're going: the big city.'

'But it's miles away, and we've got no money.'

He grins. 'You don't need money when you're with barmy Jack, Charlie. And what's a few miles? We'll do it in three or four days.'

'*Three or four days?*'

'Easy. Come on.'

CHAPTER THIRTY-THREE

'Hey Jack, where's the flipping road?' We've put the woods between ourselves and the school and now we swing right, downhill towards Speeton. We should be on the road that links the village to the tarn.

'No road, Charlie,' says Jack. 'Rough pasture, soggy this time of year.' He looks at me. 'Put a road in, do they, right up here?'

I nod. 'Must do, it's here in two thousand and seven.'

He shakes his head. 'We don't want roads anyway: get caught straight away on a road. Open country, you and me. Ah – here we are.'

It's a dilapidated brick building, too small for a house. I glance at him.

'What is it, do we sleep here?'

He chuckles. 'We don't sleep *anywhere*, Charlie: not at night. Night's for travelling.'

'So why . . . ?'

'Wait here.' There's no door, he goes inside. The moon finds a break in the clouds, pours silver on the broken roof. I look back. Nothing moves on the tussocky slope. There's a wind, it's cold enough so I can see my breath. I watch the black doorway.

When Jack comes out he's dangling a backpack with a bedroll strapped under it. I gape.

'How the heck did *that* get there?'

There's moonlight in his grin. 'I keep it here for when I feel like a little holiday.' He laughs. '*All work and no play makes Jack a dull boy*: that's a proverb.'

'I know. What you got in there?'

He shrugs. 'Stuff. Oilskin cape, socks, flashlight. Bit of chocolate, bit of mint-cake. Might come in handy.' He pulls a face. 'Only one of everything though, I never expected a mate.'

114

I smile. '*He travels fastest who travels alone*: that's another proverb.'

He nods. 'We done proverbs with Miss Stafford. Anyway.' He shrugs into the shoulder-straps. 'We've to skirt round Speeton. Follow me, and stay close. Teachers're out by now, and Fraser's got eyes like a hawk.'

CHAPTER THIRTY-FOUR

Something's not right. We're among fields and I can see the spire of the parish church against the moon. The church is in the *old* village: the bit that's been here centuries. You can't see it till you're—

It hits me like a train. *The old part's all there is.* The rest, the modern part which makes up nine tenths of Speeton, isn't built. These marshy fields we're crossing is where Hunter's Park will be: where Mum and Dad'll buy the brand new house on Beagle Avenue I'll be born in, forty-three years from now. *And I'll have passed this way before.*

116

'What you *waiting* for?' Jack's forged ahead, swinging right to avoid the village. Now he's having to wait for me. I dislodge the weird thought with a shake of my head, put on a spurt and catch up.

'Sorry, Jack, I was miles away.'

'Not *enough* miles,' he grunts. 'I want us in the old tunnel by dawn.' He wriggles through a hawthorn hedge and I follow, snagging my hoodie about fifty times.

'Old tunnel?'

'Yes. Railway tunnel, abandoned now. I've slept in it a few times.'

I giggle. 'You really are the school nut, aren't you, Jack? It's got to be even colder than the resting shed, an old railway tunnel. *And* no bed.'

'Yes, but I'm *free* there, see? Nobody watching to make sure I'm lying on my right side.' He pulls a face. 'All my life, ever since I was a baby, there's been rules. Nothing but rules, some dafter than others. One place I was in, you had to open your boiled egg at the big end. If you cracked the little end they took it off you, and the ration was only one a week. Daft.'

We're crossing field after field. Prickly hedges

separate them, and Jack seems to know where all the gaps are. Little by little, the steeple slips by to our left. Where we're walking will be streets of houses someday, parades of shops, a super-market with a filling station. It's unbelievable. When I get back, *if* I get back, I'll be able to say, *I remember when it was all fields round here.* Nobody'll believe me but I won't mind that, because I'll be where I belong. I never knew how important that was, till now.

With the village behind us we stop for a breather and Jack says, 'I reckon we can risk a bit of road-walking now. What's the time?'

I look at my watch. 'Just after half eight.'

He nods. 'Old Two Biscuits'll have driven this way by now. With a bit of luck he thinks we're making for Aston or somewhere: opposite direction. We'll make better time on the road, but be ready to drop in the ditch if you see headlamps.'

We swing left, shoulder our way through one last hedge and jump a ditch. The ditch is full of black water, there's no way I'll drop into it, head-lamps or no headlamps, but I don't tell Jack this. Moonlight shows the road curving out of Speeton and on towards Wolverstone, many miles away. There's no traffic, even this early. We walk on and Jack's right: it's a hundred times easier than stumbling across soggy fields, even though the road's lit only by the moon.

CHAPTER THIRTY-FIVE

The cold's unbelievable. I'm in my school jumper and hoodie and I'm still frozen. It's the skirt, I think: I should've grabbed my jeans. Snag is, jeans are unknown here: I'd stick out even more than I do in my hoodie.

Another unbelievable thing is how quiet it is on the road. I mean, we're talking main road here. We've been on it twenty minutes and seen four vehicles: one coming towards us, three from behind. In my world, there'd have been about three hundred.

Neither of us has dropped in the ditch, by the way. There's overgrown hedge on our right, with elms at intervals: all we have to do is step over the ditch and crouch among the tangle. The chances of a driver spotting us are practically nil, especially since headlamps seem pretty weedy compared to what I'm used to.

Besides being cold, I'm starting to get hungry. A video loop is running behind my eyes: me on the chair in Chickwood's room, the nurse coming in from the dining room carrying a steaming plateful of shepherd's pie and mashed potato, swimming in thick gravy, with mushy peas on the side, and a bowl of treacle sponge and custard for pudding. I try to switch it off but it keeps playing, and it must be cutting-edge technology because I can *smell* that gravy.

'Jack?' He strides doggedly at my side, his eyes on the road ahead.

'What?'

'How about somma that chocolate, bit of mint-cake?'

He shakes his head, keeps walking. 'Sorry, Charlie, that's for emergencies. It isn't long since we ate.'

'Lunchtime,' I protest. 'That was *hours* ago. The others have had supper.'

'The others're in bed,' he growls, 'on their right sides, while we're having an adventure.'

'*Adventure?*' I moan. 'I don't call starving an adventure. Or freezing. Don't suppose anything's open around here?'

'Such as what?'

'Chip shop, McDonald's.'

He shakes his head again. 'No chip shops out in the country, Charlie. And I don't know McDonald's: something on *your* planet, I expect.'

'Same *planet*,' I cry. *Might as well not be*, I tell myself.

'Anyway,' says Jack, 'what would we use for money? I've got two bob, and it's got to last.'

'I've got two pounds,' I tell him. 'And some change.'

Now he stops. '*Two pounds?* You've two pounds on you, now? Show me.'

I unzip my hoodie pocket, pull out a fistful of coins. 'There.'

He peers at my open palm. 'Where's the pounds, Charlie?'

'Here, dummy.' I tease out the yellow coins with a finger.

He scoffs. 'Those aren't pounds, you clot:

pounds're *notes*. What the heck are these, anyway?' He picks up a pound, squints. It's too dark to see detail.

I have a sinking feeling. *They changed the money, didn't they? Grandma says, twenty pence: that's four shillings. Four shillings to park for half an hour.* I shove the dosh back in my pocket. 'Forget it, Jack: your two bob's all we have between us.'

He hands back my useless pound, grins. 'A collector'd pay a fortune for that stuff, Charlie. Trouble is, collectors're scarcer than chip shops out here.'

We yomp on, hiding now and then when we hear motors. The later it gets, the fewer vehicles there are. After ten, they more or less dry up.

I don't know if you've ever walked all night. It's a first for me and it's really, really awful. At first your face feels stiff, the soles of your feet burn and your calves ache. After a bit you stop noticing: a sort of numbness sets in as you start turning into a mummy or a zombie. After that you think you can go on for ever, plonking one dead foot in front of the other. Nothing makes any difference. You don't know what time it is or care

123

if it rains, don't notice your surroundings at all. It's like you're trogging through a fuzzy grey tunnel where nothing matters and there's no ending.

I'm like that when Jack's voice breaks through. 'Righto, Charlie, milk bar's open.'

CHAPTER THIRTY-SIX

'Huh? What *time* is it?'

He laughs. 'You're the one with the watch.'

'Oh, yeah.' I *told* you I was a zombie. I pull my sleeve up. Five past four. Five past four *a.m.* I groan. 'What you on about, *milk bar*?'

'There.' I look where he points. We're at the start of a farm track. There's a thick, rough table standing in long grass. On it are two silver cans with lids and handles, about a metre tall.

''S not a *milk bar*,' I snarl. I'm starving, in no mood for jokes.

'It is as far as we're concerned,' he says.

'How d'you mean? It's just a couple of big tins on a table.'

'Oh, lor'.' He looks at me. 'Don't tell me you don't know what's *in* 'em.'

I shake my head, which feels like it's stuffed with cotton-wool. 'No I don't, how would I?'

'*Milk*, you dozy devil,' he hoots. 'How do farmers get their milk to market on *your* planet?'

I scowl at him. 'They're full of *milk*, out here in the middle of nowhere?'

'Certainly, why not?'

'Do the tops come off?'

'Yes.'

'Well, what's to stop somebody putting handfuls of muck in, or a dead mouse or something?'

Jack looks at me. 'Why would anyone want to do a thing like *that*, Charlie? It's *milk*. Babies drink it.' He frowns. 'Do people do that sort of thing where *you* come from?'

'I come from *here*, Jack. Different time, that's all. And yes they do, some people.'

'Why, for goodness' sake?'

I shrug. 'Dunno. Some people're *like* that, that's all I can tell you.'

'They're barmy, then.' He shrugs out of his

pack, rests it on the verge, undoes a strap. 'So what happens about the milk: in your time, I mean?'

'It's in a big tank at the farm, and when the tanker comes it's pumped straight in. It's got to be dead clean, see? If not, they won't take it.'

Jack shakes his head. 'You mean tanker like a *petrol* truck?'

'Exactly like that.'

'Wow. Anyway.' He pulls a tin mug out of his pack. 'There's our milk bar, here's a cup. Watch the track.'

He clambers onto the table, grasps the lid of a can and twists. It turns and he lifts it clear.

I look up at him. 'You're *pinching* some.'

'Yeah, sorry.' He puts the lid on the table, grabs the mug, dips it in the can. 'Nobody misses a pint of so, nobody suffers. I've done it loads of times. Here.' He hands down the mug. 'Drink up: it isn't eggs and bacon, but it might be all we get for a while.'

I drain the mug, wipe my lips with the back of a hand. Jack refills it and drinks, up there on the table. Nothing stirs on the track, and the road is quiet. When he's finished he replaces the lid, gets down and grins at me.

'Feel better now?'

I nod. 'A bit, but it's not right, you know, it's just as bad as dropping muck in.'

'No it's *not*.' He's really indignant. 'If you drop dirt in you spoil the whole churn, it has to be poured away. And you've done it for no reason. We drank because we were hungry, and what we took is neither here nor there. I bet they'll slop more on the floor of the dairy than we've just drunk. In fact, we've lowered the level a bit so it's less likely to spill.'

I have to laugh, even though I'm shattered. 'You saying we did 'em a favour?'

'No, Charlie: we done *ourselves* a favour. We done 'em no harm, that's all.'

He stows the mug, shoulders his pack and we move off. Two minutes later a truck passes us with churns on the flatbed. Jack watches it pass, pulls a face. 'We drank in the nick of time, Charlie.'

I nod. 'Yes, well that's where I've landed up, isn't it: in the nick of time.'

CHAPTER THIRTY-SEVEN

'We've to climb this wall,' says Jack. It's half past five, soon start getting light. I look over the wall. The ground falls away steeply to a railway cutting. I follow the track with my eyes. A hundred metres up it's swallowed by the mouth of a tunnel.

'Is that where we sleep?'

He nods. 'That's the kip, nice and safe.'

'What about trains?'

'I told you, it's a disused line.'

'Oh, yeah.' I yawn. 'Not at my brightest this morning, Jack.'

'Not surprised.'

We climb the wall, scramble down the embankment. Slide on our bums, actually. Once down I can see how rusty the rails are. 'Walk on the sleepers,' says Jack, 'the ballast shifts a bit.'

'I want to be one of these,' I murmur.

'One of *what*?'

I smile. 'Sleeper.'

'Ha-flippin'-ha,' goes Jack. 'You will be, wait and see.'

We reach the tunnel. Inside, the air feels damp and there's a weird pong. I wrinkle up my nose.

'Poooh, what's *that*?'

''S nothing Charlie, just old soot.' Jack's peering at the strip of ground between the track and the tunnel wall. 'Ah, here we are.'

'What were you looking for?'

'Spot I cleared last year: no lumps of ballast to dig into our backs. Hang on.'

He squats, unstraps the bedroll, spreads it on the ground. There's a thin mattress to lie on and a thinner blanket for a cover. I'm half a second from asking why he hasn't got a li-lo, or at least a man-size polybag, when the answer hits me. Of course: li-los don't exist and there's no such thing as polythene. This is roughing it, 1952 style.

'It's draughty in here,' I murmur, eyeing the blanket.

Jack nods. 'We spread the oilskin cape on top of the blanket, Charlie, it's pretty good for keeping draughts out.'

I nod. 'Sorry to keep whining, you must feel like strangling me. It's just – we've all gone soft by the millennium, Jack: central heating, fast food twenty-four seven, everything wrapped in plastic. Soft.'

'Well, Charlie.' He straightens up, looks at me. 'I understood about *half* of that, but whatever you've got up there in two thousand and seven, this'll have to do for now. It's meant for one of course: we'll be a bit snug but we'll manage.'

I don't expect to sleep: two inches of padding on hard ground and a lad's elbow in my ribs, but I do. Walk all night and you'll sleep anywhere: that's how it seems to go.

CHAPTER THIRTY-EIGHT

'Sit down, Mr Newberry, Mr Fraser. Have you both had breakfast?'

'Yes thank you, Miss Carrington.'

'Good. No fun this time of year, driving around all night. I take it neither of you saw any sign of our absconders?'

'None, unfortunately. We think they've probably spent the night hiding in a barn or out-house not far from here. Jack Lee wanders all over the countryside: he'll know a few good hidey-holes. We're pretty sure they'll be on the move anytime now, but their direction's anyone's guess.'

'Oh, I think we can be fairly sure of their direction, gentlemen. Where do we find our runaways, nine times out of ten?'

'We usually find they've gone home, Miss Carrington, but *this* is Jack Lee's home. He's got nowhere else to go. That's why we've never managed to catch him when he's gone off before: he travels at random and comes back when his empty belly's hurting him more than my cane will.'

'Yes, but Jack's always gone off by *himself*, Mr Fraser. This time he's taken Joyce Ingham with him, and she'll certainly head for home.'

'Are we absolutely certain they're together, Headmistress?'

'Oh yes. Somebody unlocked Nurse Chickwood's door from the outside, then put the key back on its nail. It wouldn't surprise me if Joyce Ingham persuaded the boy to help her leave Cold Tarn. She has the makings of a plausible rogue.'

'So you think they'll both head for Wolverstone?'

'I'm sure they will, Mr Newberry, though quite what Jack Lee imagines the Inghams will do with

133

him is beyond me. Anyway, we'll arrange things so that I'm in Pearlman Street when they arrive. I need to talk to that girl's parents in any case.'

'And in the meantime, is there anything . . . ?'

'In the meantime, Mr Fraser, Miss Parmenter and I will cover your classes while the two of you get some much-needed sleep.'

'Thank you, Headmistress.'

CHAPTER THIRTY-NINE

I wake up bursting to pee. Jack's snoring like a pig. Looks like dusk outside. I ease my arm out of the covers and squint at my watch. Twenty to four. If I can get up without waking him I'll have the privacy I need.

I shuffle sideways off the thin mattress, get to my feet without rattling the ballast too much. Jack snores on. It's perishing. We're only about ten metres into the tunnel. I creep a bit further in, to where it starts getting dark, and squat. This is the one time a skirt beats jeans. I keep my eye on the hump of bedding, but Jack doesn't stir.

Twenty to four. We've managed nearly ten hours' sleep. Still, no point waking him yet, we won't move before dark. I tiptoe along to the tunnel mouth and look out. There's the track we walked along, the road bridge, the embankment we slithered down. Something moves and I draw back. Two bobbing heads beyond the wall, guys going by. Neither looks this way. As they pass from sight a street lamp comes on, pretty weak, probably gas. Means we won't be here much longer now though.

I'm so hungry I feel sick. I'm just wondering if I can get at the sweets in the backpack without disturbing Jack, when he sits up.

'Charlie?' He's looking straight at me but I'm a silhouette: could be anyone.

''S' OK, Jack, I was just having a look. Dark soon.'

'Yes.' He gets up. 'Have another look, will you, while I see to a little job here.'

I laugh, turn away, feel him watching me every second. 'OK,' he says after half a minute. I walk back to him.

'I'm starving, thirsty too. I'd call it an emergency.'

His turn to laugh. 'Is it heck. We'll have a swig of water though, and one square of mint-cake each. Can't have you passing out on me.' He produces an aluminium bottle with a screw-cap that's fastened to its neck by a short chain. He unscrews it and passes it up. It's full, and I drink greedily till he yells, 'Whoa!' When I hand it back, he takes two little sips like a humming-bird and replaces the cap. There's an expression on his face like Miss Carrington's when New-berry ate two chocolate biscuits. I giggle, can't help it.

''S all right you laughing,' he growls. 'I've got the job of keeping us both alive till we get to Wolverstone, and it won't be easy on two bob.'

'I know, Jack,' I say, 'but *water*: England *drowns* in water all year round, know what I'm saying? We're not crossing the flipping Sahara here.'

Instead of replying he snaps a strip of mint-cake off the slab, breaks it in two. 'Here.' It's not even a mouthful but it tastes terrific. I know I ought to nibble, make it last, but I lack the willpower. I shove it in and crunch, thrilling at the way the cold/hot peppermint sensation sears my mouth and nose: distilled cleanliness. It's gone in ten seconds, but so what?

Jack nibbles his like a cockroach, then we pack our swag and stride out into the dark.

CHAPTER FORTY

Jack says, 'We need to get off this road as soon as we can.' We've scaled the embankment and climbed the wall: we're under the gaslamp on the bridge.

I glance both ways along the Wolverstone road. 'Won't they have checked this out already?'

'Oh yes, but they'll do it again. It's the way home for you, or they think it is. Runaways always go home.'

'So, where do we start going cross-country?'

'Not yet. There's a town, Yellenhall, half a mile ahead. It's got a chip shop that opens Thursday teatimes. If we put a spurt on, and with a bit of luck, we'll catch it before it shuts.'

'You're going to use your two bob with *three* days to go?'

He shakes his head. 'Not *all* of it, you fathead. Two bags of chips: fourpence.'

'Oh, wow!' I laugh. 'In *my* time, two bob's called ten pence and it'll get you about a tenth of a bag.'

'Must all be robbers in your time then.'

We set off at a good clip, energized by the prospect of food. Two men in overalls pass us going the other way, and we overtake an old guy walking his dog. They take no notice of us. We see nobody else till the road becomes Yellenhall's high street.

I smell fish and chips before we reach the shop, which is down a side street. The door's open, but there are no customers. Behind the counter a man in a white hat is wiping down his range. 'He's closing,' grunts Jack. 'Hope he's not sold out.' I hope so too: I'm slavering like a rabid dog.

'Yes, lad?' Our arrival seems to irritate the guy, like, *just when I've cleaned the place up.*

'Two bags of chips please,' goes Jack, 'and can we have some scraps on?'

'Chips?' He looks affronted. *Just* chips?'

Jack shakes his head. 'No, scraps as well please.'

The guy turns away and fills two little bags with chips, shaking his head and muttering to himself. He tops off the bags with scraps of batter, which is nice of him considering there's no charge for these and we're only spending coppers. Jack takes the bags, hands one to me and proceeds to souse his own with free vinegar and a blizzard of complimentary salt. The guy watches till he's finished, then says, 'Would you like a couple of quid out of my wallet and all, you cheeky young bogger?' I'm so embarrassed I take hardly any condiment.

Not that it spoils my appetite. We walk about a metre before leaning on the wall and cramming our mouths. It's a good job the side street's poorly lit, we must be a disgusting sight. I suck the empty bag, for goodness' sake.

'That was nice,' chirps Jack as we walk on.

I nod. 'Scrummy.' Savouring the warm tight feeling in my stomach, trying not to wonder how long it's got to last.

Little by little the buildings thin out, till Yellenhall's behind us. There are few vehicles and no pedestrians, just the road ahead and a raw, damp night.

CHAPTER FORTY-ONE

Just out of Yellenhall we leave the road but stay close to it, walking on the margins of sticky winter fields with a hedge or a fence to our left. If it's a hedge we ignore vehicles on the road and keep walking. Where it's a fence, we crouch in the dead grass and keep still till they go by. Jack knows what's safe to do, he's done it all before.

We don't talk much. He's used to his own company and I've got plenty to think about. Too much, actually. Like, how can I be here when my mum's not even born, and will I ever see her again? I think about the rest of my family too of course, and Pip. I don't half wish Pip and I had chosen to go somewhere other than Cold Tarn Woods on Monday, but then it's no good wishing, is it? And if we had gone somewhere else, would Jack be trudging across this field in the middle of the night? Was he here on 7 February, 1952, at nine-thirty in the evening, and if he was, who was with him? Wasn't *me*, was it?

See, it isn't so much missing your *mum* that screws you up in a timeslip, it's thinking about stuff like *that* that does your head in, and it doesn't get you anywhere because there are no answers. How can there be, when you find yourself wondering what'd happen if you went up to your grandparents, who must be kids right now, and said to them, *Hi, I'm the granddaughter you'll have one day, after you marry each other and have my mum and she grows up and gets married and has me*. I mean, I might not be ready for the loony-bin yet, but I soon would be if I let that stuff fester in my head. So I concentrate on missing Mum instead, and wishing I was at home in my warm bed, and wondering where Jack and I will hole up in the morning.

I ask him this and he says, 'Boat.'

'Boat? The sea's fifty miles away.'

He shrugs. 'It was fifty miles away at teatime, but we found cod.'

There's no answer to that.

I don't feel like giving a blow-by-blow account of our hike that night. It was cold, boring and incredibly long, and nothing important happened. I don't even know how many miles we walked, except it was too many.

When greyish smears are in the eastern sky, we come to a reservoir. We climb a wall and walk beside the water. I can hear little chinking noises, like somebody tapping a bottle with a fork.

'What's that?'

Jack smiles. 'Boats.'

'How d'you mean, boats? Sounds like . . .'

'It's rigging lines hitting masts, look.'

There's just enough light to make out a few small boats, high and dry, listing to port or to starboard, their masts jutting at various angles.

'Yep.' We approach a craft which is almost overgrown with long grass and has cracked, blistered varnish. 'Been here years, this one,' says Jack. 'Never moves.' He clambers onto the tilted deck, helps me up. There's a miniature wheelhouse whose door hangs by a single hinge, a hatch with a ladder. Jack nods to the ladder.

I hesitate. 'Is it all right?'

He laughs. 'Well it isn't going to sink, is it?'

He goes down, strikes a match, lights a candle. I follow. We're in a tiny cabin with a crazy canted floor, two narrow bunks and a locker where the candle stands. Nothing else. It smells fusty, but better than last night's tunnel and we've got a bed each.

He has the blanket and the bunk that slopes the wrong way, I get the mattress and the oilskin. Not enough, but at least there's no draught. We drink the bottle dry (there's a reservoir outside), blow out the candle and close our eyes.

I sleep like a rat.

CHAPTER FORTY-TWO

Jack has to wake me at dusk. The days are short, but still I'm surprised how well I'm sleeping in these crude beds. He's been out, washed his hands and face in the reservoir, filled the water bottle. There's nobody about.

My turn. I'm not keen to splash freezing water on myself, but he's lent me his scrap of towel so I better show willing. Cold water's probably nothing to fifties folk, but give me a basinful of hot by a sizzling radiator every time.

The boats're handy for hiding among when there's no proper lavatory, and I climb back aboard feeling good. Shame about the aromas of fresh coffee and bacon, but you can't have everything.

Packing, Jack says, 'The Ingham residence tomorrow, bit of luck.'

'*Tomorrow?* You said three or four days.'

He grins. 'I know. I didn't want you to think it was going to be easy, so I exaggerated a bit.'

I snort. 'It *hasn't* been easy: my feet're like raw mince.'

He grins again. '*Now* who's exaggerating?'

I am a bit, but my feet are definitely tender as we leave the reservoir and take to the fields once more. I'm relieved to think this might be our last night out, and that it won't be long before we prove once and for all that I'm not Joyce Ingham. Worries stir as to what might be waiting for us after: slippers and canes and goodness knows what, but I stick them on the back burner.

On the front burner is food. I suppose at other times of year you'd find stuff in the countryside: apples, turnips, plums. Jack would, certainly. But it's February. Orchards're bare, fields ploughed up, birds've pecked the last berries from the hedgerows.

I groan. Jack glances at me. 'What's up?'

'My belly thinks my throat's cut.'

He nods. 'Mine too.'

'I don't suppose there's a village with . . .'

'A chip shop, no. Nearest village is about four miles and it's got nothing. Nothing for *sale*, I mean.' He smiles. 'Might be lucky and *find* something though.'

I shoot him a suspicious glance. 'Do you mean *find*, Jack?'

He shrugs. 'You find something, somebody's lost it, haven't they?'

I'm not sure what he means, and I'm too hungry to go into it so I don't say anything. We move on.

It takes us an hour and a quarter to reach Drybrook. That's the village and Jack's right: everything's shut. There isn't even a pub: maybe that's how come *Dry*brook. It's really, really peaceful though, and I hope the residents're making the most of it, because—

– in 2005 they open a theme park here: BATMAN'S KINGDOM. *That* wakes 'em up, I can tell you: me and Pip've been and it's *loud*. We're talking permanent ear-damage.

The church stands on a grassy mound at the far end of the village. Jack gazes up at it.

'What?' I ask. 'We getting married or something?'

'Yes, if you like.' He smiles. 'Tell you what: I'll go make the arrangements, you wait in the bus shelter across the road. There's no buses after six o'clock.'

There's a bench in the shelter. I take the weight off my feet, watch him disappear round the foot of the mound. I haven't a clue what he's up to, except he's definitely not arranging a wedding.

It's twenty minutes before he reappears, crossing the deserted road.

'What the heck you been *doing*, Jack, I've been *frozen* sitting here.'

He winks, pats a bulge in his pack. 'Finding us some grub, Charlie.'

'In a *church*? What is it, wine and wafer?'

He shakes his head. 'It is *not*. I've got baked beans, biscuits, bully-beef. All things beginning with B.'

'Let's have a look.'

He glances up and down the street. 'Not here.

150

I'll show you when we're out of the village.'

I don't show him the message I've scratched on the shelter wall with a stone: he wouldn't get it. It says: NOTHING STAYS THE SAME.

CHAPTER FORTY-THREE

Just beyond Drybrook, there's a field with an old railway wagon in it. Jack nods towards the wagon. 'We'll eat in there. Lady called Barbara used to stable her horse in it, but it had to be put to sleep.'

I look at him as we cut across the field. 'How the heck do you know all this, Jack?'

'Ah, well.' He winks. 'That's the question, isn't it?'

He answers it when we're sitting in musty old straw, scooping cold beans out of the tin with our fingers and shoving them into our mouths. He's got a jack-knife in his pack that'll open tins in a jagged sort of way: you've to keep your fingers away from the rim. Some tramp's left a bottle on the floor and we've stuck a candle in it. It doesn't give much warmth but the light's handy.

'The children's home I was in before I got delicate is here in Drybrook,' Jack tells me. 'All us kids used to walk in a crocodile to church in the village every Sunday morning. The church has scout and guide troops.

'The troops have a trek-cart, tents, ground-sheets, spades and hatchets, billy-cans and all sorts of stuff you need when you go camping. There isn't room for it in the church hall, so it's stowed behind a curtain in what used to be a side-chapel in the church.' He grins in the candlelight. 'Churches are never locked, as you know. And I happen to know that among all this camping gear, there's always a box or two of tinned grub donated to the scouts and guides by parents and members of the congregation.'

'And you've nicked it?' I say through a mouthful of beans.

'Not *all* of it, obviously. Two tins and a packet of biscuits. I'm sure the donors wouldn't mind if they knew their gift was keeping a pair of home-less kids alive.'

I shake my head. 'Not exactly *homeless*, Jack.'

He shrugs. 'I've got no home, just a school. And yours won't be *built* for another forty-odd years: how homeless do you have to be?'

It's no use arguing, so I move on. 'This lady, Barbara, whose horse lived here: how d'you know her?'

'Ah, well, you see.' He puts down the empty bean tin, rips open the biscuits, offers the pack. They're stolen but I take one anyway. 'Barbara was a member of the congregation. She used to see us orphans at church, and she wanted to do something nice for us, so she started giving us rides on her horse after the service. There were a lot of us and only the one horse, so you'd to stand and wait your turn, but we loved it. Whisper, the horse was called. Some old misery told Barbara she was doing work on the Sabbath, and she said yes, the Lord's work. *That* shut him up.'

'So why were you sent to Cold Tarn, Jack?'

He pulls a face. 'I got this cough, wouldn't clear up. Started going thin.'

'How long ago was this?'

'It'll be three years at Easter. I hated it: missed

my mates. That's why I started running away: to come and see 'em. And it's why I want to help you: I know how you must be missing everybody.'

When he says this I burst out crying, can't help it. I need a hug but Jack's not the hugging sort. 'Here,' he growls, 'have another biscuit: they're off the ration.'

CHAPTER FORTY-FOUR

Beans and biscuits at suppertime, biscuits and bully-beef at three in the morning, all washed down with water from the reservoir. That's the story of our last night on the run. We open the bully crouching in a culvert under the road. Jack's never explored past Drybrook so he doesn't know a hidey-hole, and we're getting too near Wolverstone to risk lingering in the open. I shiver in our dank burrow.

'I'm scared, Jack.'

Jack chuckles. 'Trolls don't live in culverts, Charlie, they live under rickety bridges.'

'I'm not thinking about *trolls*,' I snap. 'I'm

thinking about Joyce Ingham's mum and dad. What if they think Joyce has been at Cold Tarn since Monday, and we turn up on their doorstep and tell 'em she hasn't? They'll go frantic.'

He nods. 'I know, and it could be worse than that. They'll have got Miss Carrington's letter telling 'em Joyce is at school. They might even have rushed over there and been told their daughter's run off with the school nutcase.'

'I'd forgotten all about the letter. I don't know if I dare go to their house, Jack.'

'You've *got* to, Charlie. We ran away so you could prove you're not Joyce. It's all been for nothing if the Inghams don't see you.'

'And what if ... look, Jack, my head's like totally messed up with all that's happened these last few days, all right? I'm not sure what's real and what isn't, so what if they come to the door and yell *Joyce!* and start hugging me and stuff? What *then*?'

He gazes at me open-mouthed, speaks slowly. 'That'll only happen if you are Joyce Ingham, Charlie. It *is* Charlie, isn't it: you haven't got me out here with some science fiction story you've invented?'

I shake my head vehemently. 'No, Jack, I haven't. I swear I haven't. It's just that I'm so confused, *nothing*'d surprise me. That's all I meant.'

'Hmmm: well, all I can say is you better be telling me the truth, Charlie, 'cause three on each hand from Fraser's no joke, and that's what I'll get when I go back.'

I nod. 'I know, Jack, and I think it's fantastic what you're doing for me, but that's another thing: *going back*. I mean, you'll go back, but what about me? When they find out I'm not Joyce, they'll know I don't belong at Cold Tarn. They won't want me back, and the Inghams certainly won't want anything to do with me: why should they? So where do I go?'

Jack shakes his head, sighs. 'I said *one thing at a time*, didn't I? Prove you're not Joyce, *then* worry about what happens after.' He pulls a face. 'I didn't realize how important *what happens after* was going to be for you: you might have been better off letting 'em believe you were Joyce Ingham.'

'No! No, I couldn't do that, Jack. I'm *me*: I couldn't have pretended to be somebody else. And they'd have found out eventually in any case.

But the thing is, I'm trapped in the wrong time and my only way back is by those stepping stones. I need to be at Cold Tarn so I can find them.'

Jack's expression grows sad, his voice gentle. 'There are no stepping stones, Charlie: we've searched. Either you saw something you *thought* were stepping stones, or you saw stepping stones that aren't there yet.'

Aren't there yet. My heart kicks me in the ribs. I look at Jack. 'You know, I never thought of that. Maybe there are no stepping stones in nineteen fifty-two, *because they're put there later.*' I sigh. 'Still means I need to stick around Cold Tarn, though.'

We bury the bully-beef tin with the biscuit-wrapper screwed up inside it, pack away the bottle and jack-knife and crawl out of the culvert. It's still pitch dark, and there seems to be no traffic. We decide to risk the road for a bit. And as we walk a little voice inside my head keeps asking: *Is this the road home, or the road to nowhere?*

CHAPTER FORTY-FIVE

We get funny looks as we trail through the sprawling outskirts of Wolverstone. For one thing it's really early: half-five, six o'clock. Nothing's open: the only light comes from street-lamps that're pretty weak, even though they're electric.

It's amazing how many people are about already, mostly guys in work clothes, riding push-bikes or on foot. I ask Jack where they're going and he says, 'Factories, dayshift. Don't say there's no factories on your planet?'

'Same planet,' I mutter for the hundredth time. 'And yes, there are factories, but people don't set off this early even on a weekday: most of 'em have cars.'

'Cars?' He looks at me. 'You mean ordinary workers?'

'Yes, practically everybody. The roads are murder at half-seven. Not on a Saturday, though.'

'Crikey: hope it's like that when I start working. It's only bosses who drive to work now: the only cars I know belong to Fraser and Newberry, and they're tin lizzies.'

When we're well into the city, Jack stops a thin woman in a shabby coat and asks after Pearlman Street. Amazingly, she knows where it is and gives directions. It's a quarter to seven, still dark.

We follow the woman's instructions and find ourselves in a maze of mean, narrow streets between rows of grimy-looking terraced houses, some of them dilapidated. There are no gardens or yards: house doors open directly on to cracked, greasy pavements. Mounds of horse droppings litter the cobbles, and here and there are stained mattresses and broken prams.

'This is a disgusting place,' I murmur.

Jack shoots me a quizzical look. 'What's it like where *you* live, Charlie: Buckingham Palace?'

'No, but ... *horse* manure.' I wrinkle up my nose.

'Horses wear nappies on your planet, do they?'

I shake my head. 'There are no horses, Jack. Not on the street. Don't you get clouds of flies?'

'In summer, yes. Don't hurt anybody, flies. Not like wasps.'

I pull a face. 'They're *filthy*, they spread diseases. No wonder you get delicate kids.'

'Yes, well, we can't all choose where to live, Charlie. Who lives here in your time?'

'There's nowhere like this in my time. It's like a picture from *Oliver Twist*.'

'So what happens to all these houses?'

'Get bulldozed, I suppose, make room for flats.'

'What the heck're *flats*?'

'You know: high-rise apartments?'

He shakes his head. 'No. So everything's bright and clean is it, in your time?'

'Well no, not exactly, but—'

'Ah!' He nods to a name-plate. 'Here we are: Pearlman Street. Now, which side's even?'

We walk on watching numbers. I'm every bit as scared as I knew I'd be. As we approach 132, the door opens and a guy lifts a bike off the step.

'Look,' hisses Jack. 'It's your dad.'

'Wish it was.' We slow down as he mounts up and wobbles away from us with his cycle-clips, flat cap and knapsack. He reminds me of Granville in that old TV show they keep re-running: *Open All Hours*. Watching him from the step is a thin girl who might be about my age. I hang back, but Jack draws level just as she turns to go in.

'Excuse me?' he says.

The girl scowls at him. 'What d'you want?'

'Is your mother in?'

I'm beside him now, looking at the girl. She's a poorly-looking thing with red-rimmed eyes.

She shakes her head. 'Mam don't live with us no more.' A toddler wriggles into view, wearing a grey vest and sucking a furry dummy. The girl clamps a hand among the child's sticky curls, snarls, 'Get *in*,' and sends it reeling out of sight.

'Your dad, then?' I just want to run, but Jack's not about to give up.

The girl nods down the street. 'That's him, gone to work. Half day Saturday, back at one.'

I chip in. 'Are you Joyce?'

She gives me a cold stare. 'What if I am?'

'You're Joyce Ingham, aren't you? You were supposed to start at Cold Tarn Open Air School last Monday.'

She shakes her head. 'Can't: who'd mind the little ones?'

'But you are Joyce, aren't you?'

'All right, yes I am. Who're you?'

'My name's Charlie, but they think I'm you. I need you to prove I'm not.'

'Charlie's a boy's name. What you talking about? *Who* thinks you're me?'

'At school. The teachers. Can we wait and see your dad? We need him to—'

'Aaah.' The girl's face clears. '*That's* why the letter says that.'

I look at her. 'Says what?'

'Say's I'm *there*, at school, being bad. Says Dad has to go there so they can talk to 'im.' She shakes her head. 'Won't go though: don't like school, my dad don't, nor teachers neither.'

Jack interrupts. 'Look, we're not bothered about you not coming to school, Joyce. All we want is for your dad to tell Miss Carrington that my mate here isn't his daughter. D'you think—?'

164

He gets no further. We're so wrapped up getting through to Joyce, we haven't noticed the car drawing into the kerb. The first we know is when a voice behind us purrs, 'Why do they *always* turn up at home, eh? The absconders, I mean. Don't they know it's the first place we'll look?'

We spin round. Fraser's on the pavement. Inside the car sits Two Biscuits, glaring at us through the windscreen.

CHAPTER FORTY-SIX

'It's *not* home sir,' I blurt, 'not *mine* anyway. *This* is Joyce Ingham.' I turn to point out the thin girl, but she's not there. The door's closed.

Fraser frowns at me. 'What the *dickens* are you talking about, girl? Why would you come here if it wasn't your home?'

'To prove I'm not Joyce Ingham, sir.'

He shakes his head. 'How could you even know this house existed unless it was familiar to you before you came to Cold Tarn?'

Jack breaks in. 'I can explain that, sir. I saw the letter Miss Carrington wrote to Joyce's parents. The envelope, I mean. We got the address off it.'

166

Fraser's pondering this when Newberry joins him. He hasn't heard what's been said. 'Why're we all standing around?' he growls. 'We should be inside the house, asking Joyce's parents why they haven't responded to the Head's letter.' He looks at me. 'Lead on, Joyce, if you please.'

I shake my head. 'I can't, sir, it's not my house. I've never been here in my life.'

'Oh nonsense, I haven't time for this.' He strides to the door, hammers on it with the side of his fist, calls out, 'Come on, come on: we know somebody's in.' He waits, and when there's no response he shouts, 'All right, if that's the way you want it, I'm quite prepared to involve the police.'

There's a brief silence, then the door cracks open and the girl peeps out. 'I *couldn't* come to school, sir,' she whines, 'due to Mum going off. Dad's got to work, and who'd mind my little sisters and baby brother?'

Two Biscuits gazes at the strip of face while he digests this. After a bit he says, 'Is your name Joyce?'

The girl nods. 'Yes.'

'Ingham: you're Joyce *Ingham*?'

'Yes, sir.'

'Then who's *this*?' He nods towards me.

Joyce opens the door a bit wider to look at me. 'Dunno, sir, I never seen 'er before.'

'So then . . .' He looks from me to Joyce and back to me. 'It's true: you're not Joyce Ingham?'

Old Two Biscuits, I think but don't say, *showcasing his swiftness on the uptake.* 'No, sir,' I say. 'That's what I've been trying to tell everybody.'

'Yes, I see.' He turns to the girl. 'All right, Joyce, it's obvious you have sound reasons for failing to turn up at Cold Tarn. We needn't trouble the police, but d'you think we might come in, try to sort something out?'

She lets us in and brews a pot of tea. When she finds out me and Jack have walked through the night we get toast, which is good of her, considering she's got three knee-biters and a baby to see to.

I don't know what happens after we eat the toast, because Jack and I fall asleep on a dead sofa that small hands have embalmed with jam. When we wake up, Joyce's dad's there, something's been decided and it's time for us to go.

Fraser installs Jack in the back seat of his tin

lizzie, then turns to me. 'Well, Charlotte: it seems your presence at Cold Tarn really is the result of a mistake, but what do you plan to do now?'

I shake my head. 'I don't know, sir, there's nowhere I can go. It's the wrong time, you see. I *know* nobody believes me, but it's true.'

'Hmmm.' He sighs. 'Well, I can't say what will be done with you in the long term, but I think for now you ought to come back to school: at least you'll be fed and have a roof over your head.' He smiles. 'No walls, mind, just the roof.'

Probably a decent guy, old Fraser.

CHAPTER FORTY-SEVEN

It's Saturday, but Miss Carrington's in her study. You have to be dedicated to teach at a place like Cold Tarn. She stands up as Fraser ushers me and Jack in. Newberry's there already: we've showered and changed, and he's brought the Head up to speed.

It's nothing like I'd pictured it, our return. I expected anger, shouting, severe punishment for the pair of us. Instead, Carrington seems pleased to see us. The biscuit tin's out and Newberry's looking smug: I bet he's had two already.

'Well, Jack,' says the Head, when she's had a close look at us both. 'You seem none the worse for your adventure. You've had lots of practice of course, though not with a companion. However,' she smiles, 'you seem to have taken good care of Charlotte.'

Jack nods. 'I done my best, miss.'

'*Did*,' corrects the head, automatically. 'You *did* your best, Jack.'

'Yes, miss.'

'Mmmm.' She looks him in the eye. 'For once, you had a good reason for absconding and you won't be punished. But – and it's a big but, Jack – you must *never* run away again. Mr Newberry and Mr Fraser have spent quite enough time these past three years chasing you across the landscape like a game of cops and robbers. I expect they'll both be very angry if they ever have to do it again.' She turns to them. 'Am I right, Mr Newberry?'

'You certainly are, Headmistress.'

'Mr Fraser?'

'Oh yes, Headmistress: I shall be very, very angry. In fact I doubt whether I'll be able to control my right arm.'

'That's your caning arm, is it not, Mr Fraser?'

'It is indeed, Headmistress.'

I think they're kidding: hamming it up. *Must* be, surely. Anyway, Jack's expression signals he's got the message and he departs with the two men, leaving me alone with Carrington.

'Now, Charlotte.' She's back behind her desk. 'It seems I owe you an apology. You're *not* Joyce Ingham, and I'm sorry I refused to believe you about that: sorry you had to run away in order to prove it.'

I don't know how to respond to this. I suppose it'd be polite to say *it's all right*, but it isn't. It's not all right to assume someone's lying. I remember some words from an old film: *If you can't say something nice, don't say anything at all.* I stay quiet.

The Head sits back, sighs. 'The thing is, we're no further forward really. You've proved who you're not, but not who you are. Oh, I don't mean your name: it's Charlotte Livingstone, but where has Charlotte Livingstone come from? Where ought she to be at this very moment? People somewhere are missing you, Charlotte: they worry, wonder where you are. I don't think you *know* who you are, do you?'

I meet her gaze, speak quietly. 'I wish my

answers were easier to believe, miss, because they're true. As true as my name.'

She shakes her head. 'Have you heard of amnesia, dear?'

I shake mine.

'It means loss of memory,' she continues. 'It happens to lots of people. A bang on the head can bring it on. You'd fallen when I found you in the grounds last Monday: perhaps you banged your head.' She rabbits on so I've no chance to butt in. 'Sufferers forget everything: name, address, family, job: all wiped clean They wander about bewildered, till somebody notices and takes them to hospital. Then it usually comes back, bit by bit.' She smiles. 'I think you've got amnesia, Charlotte. I think if we keep you here, look after you, your memory will come back, bit by bit.' She beams. 'After all, you remembered your name straight away.'

CHAPTER FORTY-EIGHT

I want to argue of course. Carry on the struggle. I'm dying to say, *You thought I was lying about my name, but I wasn't. You were wrong about that and you're wrong about everything else: especially amnesia.*

I can't though, can I? Think about it. I'm not Joyce Ingham, so I don't belong at Cold Tarn. I'm not one of their pupils: they're not responsible for me. They can chuck me out any time, *then* what do I do? Nothing to eat, nowhere to sleep. They might even take back the warm clothes they gave me, turn me loose in jeans and hoodie, and it's February. Without Jack and

174

his survival techniques I'd be dead in a week.

Truth is, they're letting me stay out of the kindness of their hearts. There are other truths, but right now *that*'s the one that counts. If Miss Carrington wants to believe I've lost my memory, I'll play along in exchange for food and shelter. There are worse bargains. I'll play along, and hope that sooner or later I'll find the stepping stones that'll take me home.

The Head's watching me across her desk. She smiles. 'Sunday tomorrow, dear: you can have a nice long rest before you rejoin Miss Stafford's class on Monday. You remember Miss Stafford, don't you?'

'Yes, miss.' *It's only been three days, of course I remember.*

'Splendid. Well.' She rubs her hands together. 'While you're studying geography with Miss Stafford, I'll be making enquiries about missing persons.' She smiles. 'As I said, somebody somewhere is looking for you, Charlotte: we'll reunite you with your loved ones sooner or later, and in the meantime we'll take good care of you. Off you go dear: you're just in time for supper.'

This is going to sound weird, but when I walk

into the dining room and take my place at Cissy Murgatroyd's table, it feels like coming home. Nine familiar faces: eighteen eyes shining with eagerness to hear the story of my adventure. Or so I think, till Kenneth Trubshaw speaks for all of them.

'How many did she give you, Joyce? Does it hurt to sit down?'

No change here, then. I breathe in slowly, my voice is calm. 'It's not Joyce, it's Charlotte. Charlie if you like. Joyce is in Wolverstone, being Mary Poppins. She might show up later. Miss Carrington didn't give me *any*: she knows I had a good reason for bunking off. Sorry to disappoint.'

Martin Kent shrugs. ''S all right, Charlie, we don't mind.' He grins. 'You can tell us something else instead. What was it like, being by yourself with barmy Jack Lee for three days?'

'And *two nights*?' adds a girl called Renee.

I smile. 'It was absolutely fine. Jack's not the nut you take him for. He knows a lot of stuff about getting grub and finding shelter. Survival techniques.'

'Hoooo!' goes Cissy. '*Survival techniques*. Charlie must've swallowed a dictionary.' Her bruises have faded to nothing.

Kenneth nods. 'Probably all Jack could find to eat out there.'

Everybody laughs. I don't mind, and I know Jack wouldn't either: he doesn't give a stuff what *anybody* thinks. I glance across to his table. He's looking, wondering what they're laughing at. I smile at him. He nods and smiles back and I feel a warm glow. It's a good job there's Jack: I don't think I'd cope without him.

Supper's cheese pie and mushy peas, which inspires jokes about trumping in the dorms. It seems *trump*'s a really bad word in 1952: kids lower their voices when saying it, glance all round in case a teacher's listening. It's the same with various other words: words me and Pip use all the time. This is one of the thousand little things that pop up every minute of every day, making it impossible for me to forget I'm among strangers.

Those words I scratched in the bus shelter at Drybrook – NOTHING STAYS THE SAME. They're probably the truest words I'll ever write.

CHAPTER FORTY-NINE

Sunday I lie in. Means missing breakfast but it's worth it. One thing about kipping on ballast in a railway tunnel: it makes a narrow bed in a room with three walls seem cosy.

Around eleven I start wondering what Jack's doing, so I get up. It's cold and windy, so the grounds are deserted and the recreation hut's like the black hole of Calcutta. You can't get near the radio, all the ludo boards're taken and Mr Fraser's organized a waiting-list for table tennis. The only kid missing is Jack.

I haven't a clue where to start looking for him, so I ask Cissy. She pulls a face. 'He'll have gone somewhere that's out of bounds, Charlotte: he usually does.'

'What sort of places are out of bounds?'

'Oh, you know – dangerous places.'

'The tarn?'

'No, that's in bounds. The Red Lion in Speeton's out of course, and the railway line; the electricity pylon in Tuke's field and the old quarry. Oh, and any field that happens to have a bull in it.' She smiles. 'Boys like to play Cap and Bull, you see.'

'What's Cap and Bull?'

'You snatch somebody's cap and throw it as far as you can into a field where there's a bull. The owner daren't come back to school without his cap, so he has to go and fetch it while his friends wave and yell to alert the bull.'

'With friends like those . . .' It's a quote you never complete, right? You don't *need* to, because everybody knows it, but Cissy blanks me. 1952 strikes again.

'Out of those,' she continues, 'I'd bet on the quarry. It's a favourite haunt of Jack's.'

'Where is it?'

She shakes her head. 'Don't go, Charlotte. The

179

staff turn a blind eye for Jack because he's a bit of a favourite, but you'd be in hot water: especially straight after running away. He'll be back for lunch anyway.'

I go down towards the classrooms and walk about on the grass. I tell myself it's to keep warm while waiting for Jack to come back, but it isn't. I'm looking for stepping stones: I want to go home.

I don't know it, but while I'm wasting my time looking for something that isn't there, Jack's busy unearthing the object that'll end up giving me my one slim chance.

CHAPTER FIFTY

It's twenty past twelve when I spot him coming towards me. There's something funny about his walk. As he gets closer, I see he's carrying a great slab of stone. I call to him.

'What you got there, Jack: your gravestone?'

'Would be,' he gasps, 'if I'd to hump it much further.' He staggers past me and drops it near Newberry's classroom. It's yellowish, flat, roughly oval in shape. I look from it to him. 'How far've you carried this, Jack?'

He shrugs. "Bout half a mile, Charlie. With rests.'

I shake my head. 'Doesn't look worth it.'

'That's 'cause it's landed wrong way up. Watch.'

He squats, slides the fingers of both hands under the slab and lifts it onto its edge. It topples and slams down and there's a shape on this side, like somebody pressed a giant sycamore leaf into it when it was soft.

Jack straightens up, grinning and rubbing his hands. 'There.'

I look at the shape. 'What is it?'

'Footprint.'

'Yeah, right.' I nod. 'But what is it really, Jack?'

'I told you, it's a footprint. A *dinosaur* footprint.'

I'm gob-smacked. I mean, I know people've found footprints: I've seen 'em on telly, seen 'em behind glass in museums. But I never *knew* anybody who found one, never had one right in front of me where I could touch it.

I look at Jack. 'Where'd you find it?'

'Quarry. Abandoned quarry, loads of fossils. Never seen one of these before, though.'

I smile. 'P'raps the dinosaur made it last night.'

He shakes his head, serious. 'No, Charlie, it's been there all the time. Millions of years. *Millions.*' He squats, traces the edge of the shape

182

with a finger. 'I'm the first living thing to touch this since the dinosaur lifted its foot clear, all that time ago.' His voice is full of wonder, and this combines with a fleeting facial expression to deliver a jolt to my heart. I don't know how else to describe it: it's a jolt, and it leaves behind a feeling that Jack and I have met before. Not here but *like* this: sharing wonder. Doesn't last long, but it's the weirdest sensation while it does.

I talk to cover my confusion. 'Fingers didn't exist,' I point out, 'only toes. What were the odds, back then, against this particular footprint being touched someday by a finger? Millions to one, I'd say.'

'Billions.' He looks up. 'You know, Charlie, we think the same barmy thoughts. I reckon you're as nutty as I am. I wish—'

'What?'

'I wish I'd had you with me at Cold Tarn from the start. We'd've had loads of adventures: loads of fun, 'cause we're the same.'

'I know, I was thinking that as well.' I hesitate, then add, 'I still want to go home, though.'

He nods. 'Course you do. *I* would, if I had one.'

This is getting heavy. I change the subject. 'What you gonna do with this?' I nod at the slab.

'Show it to old Two Biscuits.' He chuckles. '*Wonderful* nickname, that. You're a genius, Charlie. Mad keen on fossils, he is. Might even get a gold star in my book.'

I laugh. 'You deserve a gold star for just humping it, specially since you're delicate.'

'Delicate my foot,' he scoffs. 'It's jam roly-poly today: I'll race you.'

Old Jack: he's about as delicate as a wrecking ball.

CHAPTER FIFTY-ONE

Newberry's off the premises Sunday, so it's Monday morning before Jack shows him the footprint. It's worth the wait though: the guy's like a kid on its birthday. We're supposed to have geography with Miss Stafford, but Newberry insists that both she and Mr Fraser bring their pupils to join his own in gawping at the slab while he gives a little talk.

It's funny really. In 2007, any *kid* could've given that talk. I mean, everybody does dinosaurs at school, plus there's books and films and travelling exhibitions, all about dinosaurs. By the time you're nine, you've got dinosaurs coming out of your ears.

Not so, it seems, in 1952. Old Two Biscuits has gathered up everything he can find on dinosaurs, and it amounts to a few mentions in encyclopaedias and dictionaries, illustrated by boring, black and white pictures. Some of the kids have never even heard of dinosaurs.

All this changes over the next few days. Just because pupils are ignorant doesn't mean they're not interested. Turns out they're every bit as interested in dinosaurs as kids usually are, and all three teachers seize on this enthusiasm to get the children working.

Take Miss Stafford. She doesn't drag us back to geography when we've finished looking at Jack's find. She's like, *One footprint: one. Now who can tell me where else we come across a single footprint: just one, and no sign of the foot that left it?*

I haven't a clue. It's a while before anybody has. Miss Stafford waits, twinkling, while we rack our brains. It's Kathleen Rayner who cracks it in the end. 'Please, miss, *Robinson Crusoe.*'

'Excellent, Kathleen. And whose footprint is it?'

Trubshaw's hand shoots up. 'Yes, Kenneth?'

'Miss, Robinson Crusoe's.'

'No. Yes, Martin?'

'Man Friday's, miss.'

'Correct. So.' Her eyes sweep across the faces in front of her. 'Suppose we want to give our dinosaur a name: what might be a good one? Yes, Susan?'

'Man Friday, miss.'

'Yes, or Friday for short. But why did Robinson Crusoe name his companion Friday?'

'Miss, because it was a Friday when he rescued him from the cannibals.'

'Right, and what day was it when we saw our footprint?'

'Today, miss: Monday. We could call him Monday.'

'We could indeed, Susan, in fact we *will*.' She smiles. 'Of course, *he* might have been *she*, but it doesn't matter: Monday will do for either, like . . . like Charlie.' She smiles at me and I feel myself blush.

Once we've got the name sorted, Miss Stafford gets us talking about what Monday might have *looked* like: size, shape, colouring. In my world, we'd have based our mind-pictures on animatronics we'd seen, or illustrations, but these kids have nothing like that. All sorts of weird stuff's suggested: one footprint, so maybe one leg. She lets us punt it about a bit, then gives out paper and crayons and tells us to draw what we see in our heads.

It's like being six again. I love it. Instead of sticking to known forms I let my imagination rip, producing an impossibly hideous beast with three heads and eyes in its tail. I pinch an old joke for my title, calling it D'YOU FINK HE SORE US? I have to explain it to Miss Stafford, but she laughs when she gets it.

There's only one wall, and by naptime it's papered all over with monsters. The other classes have been doing dinosaurs as well, and the talk in the resting shed's all *this*osaurus, *that*osaurus and *theother*osaurus. Miss Paramenter has a tough time getting us settled on our right sides with our eyes closed.

This is the first step on my road home.

CHAPTER FIFTY-TWO

Tuesday's basket day. It's quite warm for once, so it feels nice sitting outside. Mr Case has done a bit of tidying up on my cuckoo's nest, and I find I'm starting to get the hang of it. Jack and I sit side by side and talk while we work.

'What's *adapt* mean, Charlie?' he asks.

'Uh . . . it's like when you change yourself to cope with something different. Like me, changing so I can handle being here in nineteen fifty-two. Why?'

'Oh, I was talking to Two Biscuits. He says the reason there's no dinosaurs now is, the climate changed and they couldn't adapt.'

'Ah, yes.' I nod. 'That's what the scientists *used* to think.'

He glances at me sideways. '*Used* to? You mean they don't in your time?'

'No.'

'What do they think, then?'

'Well, they discovered that the dinosaurs didn't die out gradually, like they would if they failed to adapt. They seem to have disappeared quite suddenly, like in a few weeks or months. And the only thing that could make that happen is some massive disaster – something that'd change the world completely in a very short time. They think a gigantic meteorite – maybe a comet – collided with the Earth.'

'What – and flattened 'em all?'

I laugh, can't help it. 'Not exactly. It caused a massive explosion, which threw millions of tons of muck into the atmosphere. The winds smeared this muck in a thick cloud right round the Earth, blotting out the sun. It got really cold. Most plants died, so the plant-eating dinosaurs starved. The meat-eaters hung on for a while, eating the dead plant-eaters. But when they'd eaten them all, they starved too. It didn't take long.'

'Wow! Wait till I tell old Newberry: he'll be the first person in the world who knows what *really* happened, apart from you and me.'

I shake my head. 'I wouldn't tell him if I were you, Jack. He'd only think I was guessing again, like with the King.'

We weave on. Just when I think we've finished with dinosaurs for today, Jack chuckles.

'You'll never guess what some dope in Newberry's class asked him.'

'What?'

'He said, *did they have dinosaurs when you were little, sir?* Then they say *I'm* barmy.'

'What did Newberry say?'

'Dunno, he didn't tell me.'

'That's much better, Charlotte,' says Case at the end of the lesson. 'We'll make a weaver of you yet.'

Leaver, I think but don't say, *not weaver*. I may be better than a dinosaur at adapting, but it's leaving I'm really interested in.

It's four o'clock, our free time. Jack says, 'today's our weekiversary, Charlie – we met by the tarn a week ago today.'

'Crikey, so we did. Seems a lot longer.'

'That's 'cause you're homesick. D'you fancy a stroll up there now, mark the occasion?'

I nod. 'If you like, as long as we don't make ourselves late for supper like last time.'

It's dusk, we follow the picket fence uphill. Jack says, 'We may be two of a kind, but we wish for opposite things, Charlie.'

'How d'you mean?'

'Well, I wish you'd stay for ever, and you just want to go back.'

'Yes, it's true I want to go back. Didn't know you wished I'd stay for ever, though.' I look at him. 'You know Sunday, when you flipped that slab over?'

'Yes I do, what about it?'

'I had the weirdest feeling, like we'd done it before, or something like it. Long time ago.'

He shakes his head. 'Impossible, Charlie.'

'I know. It was just for a second, but it got to me. I keep thinking about it.'

'Yes, it *is* weird.' He grins. 'You don't think it means we'll get *married* someday, do you?'

'We probably will, you know.'

'Huh? You really think so?'

'Yeah. But not to each *other*.'

CHAPTER FIFTY-THREE

After morning nap Thursday Jack says, 'Hey, Charlie: come and see what old Two Biscuits has done with my footprint.'

'It isn't *your* footprint,' I tell him. 'You'd never get your shoe on.'

'Ha-flippin'-ha. Come on.' He sets off across the lawn.

'Where we going?' I protest. 'We'll miss lunch.'

'Will we hummer, only be a minute.'

We're near the fence when he stops. The slab's at his feet. A section of turf has been cut and removed and the slab dropped in, so that it lies flush with the ground. It's like fitting the last piece into a jigsaw puzzle.

'Looks really neat,' I say, 'but why put it right out here?'

'That's what *I* thought,' growls Jack, disgruntled. 'What's wrong with putting it near the classrooms, where people can see it? Hardly anybody comes past here.'

I pull a face. 'Ask him, Jack. You found the thing, he can't blame you for wanting to know.'

He nods. 'P'raps I will, Charlie, next time I see him.'

We stroll across to the dining room. Here and there, clumps of crocus thrust through the grass to mark with purple, white and yellow the approach of a long-ago spring that has nothing to do with me. Mum's crocuses'll be out now: her favourite flowers, but this year she won't even notice them 'cause her daughter's missing. Given up for dead, probably, like most girls who vanish.

Nurse Chickwood's hanging about outside the dining room. I know the second I spot her she's waiting for me. Doesn't help cheer me up, I can tell you.

'Ah, Charlotte.' Jack and I stop, she looks at Jack. 'You go along, dear, I just need a word with Charlotte.' Jack gives me a questioning look, moves on.

'Now, Charlotte.' Chickwood keeps her voice low. 'Miss Carrington has made enquiries in various quarters to try to discover who might be missing you, and nothing's come up. She will keep trying of course, but it's felt that until your family is located, probably the best plan is for you to be cared for in a children's home, rather than here at school.'

'But miss—'

She cuts in, smiling. 'They've got experts, you see, dear: experts in dealing with your sort of situation, whereas what we have is a waiting-list of delicate children needing places here at Cold Tarn. With all this in mind, Miss Carrington has asked me to tell you that arrangements are being made for you to be handed over sometime in the next few days.'

'But miss, Jack's my friend, my only friend here. I've been adapting, getting used to things. It's not easy. I don't think I could stand to do it over somewhere else.'

She gives me the same smile. 'You'll make new friends in no time, Charlotte. Just think: ten days ago you'd never met Jack, now he's your friend. Run along before your dinner gets cold.'

CHAPTER FIFTY-FOUR

I go straight across to Jack's table, murmur in his ear. 'They're sending me away: children's home.'

'Oh, heck. It'll be Drybrook, where I was.'

'What's it like?'

'Not bad. Staff's not as nice as here.'

'I don't want to go, Jack.'

'Don't blame you. Dunno what to do, though.'

'Charlotte?' Cissy calls across. 'Come on, we're all starving.'

'Coming.' I squeeze Jack's shoulder. 'Talk later.'

Kent smirks at me as I slip into my place. 'When's the wedding, Charlie?'

'Lend me your brain, Martin,' I snarl, 'I want to build an idiot.' This breaks everybody up as I knew it would. In the past, you can recycle every corny crack you know and be famous for your wit. If only I was in the mood to enjoy it.

Jack and I manage a few words at nap time and in afternoon lessons, but it doesn't solve anything.

We're doing about warm-blooded/cold-blooded animals. Miss Stafford says dinosaurs were cold-blooded: they'd to wait for the sun warming them up, so they'd be slow getting started in the mornings. 'Bit like you, Martin Kent,' she says, which gets a snigger. If I could be arsed, I'd tell her some scientists now think dinosaurs were *warm*-blooded, but I don't. I'm too busy watching for a car from the children's home.

As it is, the only vehicle I see is the gardener's wreck of a van. It chugs past three times between half-two and four, which is unusual. When lessons are over, we see the guy's been carting stone slabs, there's a pile by Newberry's room. Kids form a ring round the pile, discussing it and poking the slabs with their shoe-toes.

'They're from the quarry,' says Jack, 'same as my slab. No footprints though: wonder what he wants 'em for?'

We don't find out straight away: Jack fancies a drama that's on *Children's Hour,* so we stroll up to the recreation hut and join the huddle round the radio.

It's rubbish. There's no fights, no car-chases, and talk about s-l-o-w. I don't know how they've the cheek to call it a drama. Everybody else is glued to it, mind, so maybe this is as wild as it gets in '52.

Trooping down to supper, we see that the gardener's started a path across the lawn. He's only laid three or four slabs so far, but you can see it'll run out to the main driveway. 'What's the *point?*' growls Jack. 'There's a concrete one already.'

At the supper table I say, to nobody in particular, 'I can't get used to going to bed at seven, specially when we have two naps in the day.'

'Huh!' grunts Kenneth Trubshaw. 'It's easy this time of year. Wait till the clocks go on: you lie there while the sun burns your eyeballs out.'

'She won't be here by then,' says Cissy. 'Will you, Charlotte?'

'No.' I lower my eyes, wish she hadn't said anything.

Kent pipes up straight away. 'Off back where there's no cane, I bet. Can *I* come, Charlie?'

'She's going to a children's home,' blabs Cissy, 'till her memory comes back.'

'My memory's *fine*,' I snap, furious that she has all this information.

Raymond Farr weighs in. 'Ooooh – I *heard* about that home: the cane's got nails hammered through, and there's beetles and long black hairs in the porridge.'

'You can't kid me about Drybrook, *stupid*,' I tell him. 'Jack was there.'

'Yes, and then he was sent *here* 'cause his chest was wrecked. How'd it get like that, eh?'

The words from that old film come to me again. *If you can't say something nice, don't say anything at all*, I think again. Shame they don't teach *that* at Cold Tarn.

CHAPTER FIFTY-FIVE

It all comes clear Friday morning. The path, I mean. We've got our maths books out, we're about to start, when a kid from Newberry's class sticks her head in.

'Please, miss, Mr Newberry says could everybody come outside for a few minutes, he's got something to show them.'

It's the path. Except it's not really a path. If it were, there's no way it'd be finished already, because it extends way beyond the driveway. Two Biscuits stands on the first slab, gesturing at us to gather round. We crowd in, pushing and shoving.

'The other day,' he says when we've settled down, 'a boy who shall be nameless asked me if there were dinosaurs when I was a lad.'

There's a bit of derisive laughter, and he shakes his head. 'No no no: let's be fair. *A long time ago* can mean when I was a lad: it seems a long time ago to me. But of course it's nothing compared to the time that's passed since dinosaurs walked the Earth. A stretch of time like that – millions of years – is hard for us even to imagine. So what I've done, with Mr Gort's help, is to lay out a timeline to help us imagine it.' He makes a slicing motion with the edge of his hand to indicate the dead straight line of stones he and the gardener have laid.

'As you can see, the stones are very close together at this end: in fact the first two are touching.' He smiles. 'The one I'm standing on represents now: nineteen fifty-two. The one touching it represents nineteen thirty-one, when I was a lad. The one after that is the Great War. You can see there's a small gap. There's a slightly wider gap between it and the fourth stone, which marks the Battle of Trafalgar.'

He moves, striding from stone to stone. We follow as best we can.

'I'm moving back through time now,' he says. 'Passing the Battle of Hastings to reach the Roman Occupation, and from there to . . .'

I'm distracted at this point by the appearance of a long black car on the driveway. I watch it pull up outside the main block. The kids, following Newberry, have moved on. I don't even notice. Two people get out of the car and go into the building, leaving the driver at the wheel. I don't know they've come for me, but I have a bad feeling.

The others're way over by the fence now, where the footprint is. That's the last stone in the timeline, of course. Clever guy, old Two Biscuits, but already it feels like this has nothing to do with me: I'm leaving it all behind.

A minute later I know for sure. The two people reappear with Miss Carrington and Nurse Chickwood. Three of them come my way, Chickwood heads for the girls' dorm. She's off to get my stuff.

I hurry towards the crowd, looking for Jack. Nauseous with panic, starting to sob. *I can just keep going, can't I? Climb the fence, disappear into the woods. I can't let them put me in that car. I can't.*

Suddenly there's Jack. He knows, I can see it in his face as he pelts towards me. *What's he going to do – what can he do?* He's yelling something, I can't make it out. Pointing at the stones?

'Look, Charlie.' Yes, he's stabbing his finger at the timeline. 'Don't you see – they're your *stepping* stones!'

I stand gawping, my brain won't unscramble the words. He reaches me, spins me round, shoves me at the slabs as the Head approaches. 'Go, Charlie – first stone, then the future. Don't look back.'

Of course: it's a timeline. *A timeline.* I'm bounding now, leaping, stone to stone to stone. 'Charlotte!' cries Carrington, 'where on *earth* d'you think you're going?'

'Home!' I cry with a sob in my voice. 'I'm going home, miss.'

My foot slaps the first stone and I leap with my eyes closed and all the world's hope in my heart. A slam, like hot wind, and I'm on grass, rolling. I hold my breath, open my eyes and there's the classroom floor.

Only the floor.

CHAPTER FIFTY-SIX

I can't begin to describe my feelings at that moment: the moment I know I'm home. Joy won't do: not by itself. There's fear, for one thing. Why fear? Because right by my feet in the long grass is Newberry's timeline, which leads to the nick of time. The first thing I do, the very first, is to roll clear of it.

Sadness is in there somewhere, too. A sense of something lost. It's mostly Jack, of course: such an abrupt parting. But it isn't just Jack. In a weird sort of way it's the whole thing, which is daft considering how unhappy I was in 1952. But on the whole, people were good to me at Cold Tarn

Open Air School. They did what they thought was best for me, and I thanked them by running away. Twice. And I can't even make token amends with a *thank you* card.

Sounds like I'm thinking clearly, doesn't it, there among the old floors? I'm not. These thoughts will come gradually, over the next few days. Weeks, even. At the time, my head's a chaotic jumble of emotions but one idea dominates: I've been gone twelve days, my family thinks I'm dead, I've got to reach them.

I pat myself down, feeling for my phone, but I'm in uniform and I remember: the phone's in a pocket of my hoodie, hanging in the girls' dorm. I think of the dorm as a *place*: a place I've left but which stands intact right now, a long way away, with my phone in it. The fact that the place fell to bits long ago and lies rotting under my feet doesn't cross my mind.

I trot into the woods and take the footpath downhill. It's twelve days since Pip and I walked up it: feels like a lifetime. *Grandad. How's he doing? I hope he hasn't* . . .

As Hunter's Park comes into sight, I try to think clearly. Friday morning, nine twenty-five.

Dad'll be at work. The work goes on, even when your kid's vanished. I haven't got my key: it's in the same pocket as my phone, but Mum'll be home. Unless she's at Grandma's. If she is, I'll phone her on next door's landline. If they're in next door.

When I turn onto Beagle Avenue I start running. Don't mean to, it just happens. I'm crying, hope nobody notices. Our gates're open 'cause Dad's driven off. I run up the path. Acton's at the front-room window. I wave, his mouth drops open, he disappears. I head for the side door, hear the front door open behind me. I stop, turn. Mum dashes out with her arms open, mewing. We collapse on each other and Keeper capers round, yapping.

It's madness for an hour. Acton calls Dad, he arrives like a Formula One star and we stagger across the room hugging while Mum phones Grandma, the police and everyone she knows. And of course there are the questions: *Are you all right, what happened, where've you been?*

I don't answer that one: *where've you been?* What can I say without sounding barmy? In a sense I haven't been *anywhere*, just up by Cold

207

Tarn Woods. Not somewhere, but some*when*. So I pinch Miss Carrington's idea, pretend I don't remember.

Luckily nobody pushes it. Too relieved, too happy. So determined not to spoil the occasion, they're keeping something from me. It's only when I corner Mum in the kitchen and ask her straight out, *How's Grandad?*, that she tells me.

'Your grandad died, sweetheart,' she murmurs. 'In his sleep, sometime during Wednesday night. I'm so sorry.'

Me too, Grandad.

CHAPTER FIFTY-SEVEN

Amazingly, even *that* comes out all right in the end. And I do mean amazingly. But first there are various bits of hassle I suppose I ought to have expected, but didn't.

One's about my clothes. When the first frenzy's died down and it's just us, Mum says, 'That outfit you've got on, Charlotte: it looks like a school uniform. Where'd it come from, and where're the clothes you were wearing when you . . . went missing?'

I look down at myself, doing my amnesia bit. 'Oh, I dunno. What was I wearing, Mum? I don't remember.'

'Philippa said you were in your jeans and hoodie. They're not in your room, so she must be right. What happened to them?'

I wish I could tell Mum the truth, but I can't. I *can't*. Not yet anyway. I shake my head. 'I *told* you, I can't remember. I don't remember *anything* till . . . till I came round and found myself in the woods.'

Dad chips in, gripping my shoulders, looking me in the eye. 'Did somebody touch you, Charlie: make you do something you didn't want to?'

'No, Dad, it was nothing like that.'

He frowns. 'You know the sort of thing I mean, don't you?'

I nod, look at the carpet. 'Yes,' I murmur. 'Nothing happened.'

The police come. Detective Constable Stables and Dr Randle, the police doctor. D.C. Stables asks me stuff Mum and Dad have asked already. I give the same answers: can't remember. Then I have to go upstairs with Dr Randle, and be examined. I have to take my clothes off.

She picks up the official Cold Tarn knickers and says, 'Were you wearing these when you left home, Charlotte?'

Course not, I feel like saying, *what d'you think I am?* But I just say no.

'Hmmm.' She frowns. 'It's just that they're very old fashioned, Charlotte: so's the vest. Did somebody give them to you?'

'I don't remember.'

'Mmmm.' She doesn't say anything, but I don't think she believes me.

There's other bits, when the police have gone. My door key, phone. *Couldn't you at least have called, put our minds at rest?*

Same answer. Well: I've no choice, have I? Takes some of the shine off being home, that's all.

Monday it's back to school. Not a lot of fun, but Pip's there for me as ever, no questions asked. Well, hardly any. And they give me Tuesday off for Grandad's funeral.

It's not your everyday funeral, if there is such a thing. Grandad was a humanist, and he has a humanist funeral. There's no preacher, no hymns. Instead there's the *Ode to Joy* on CD, and Nina. Nina's what's known as an officiant, and it's from her I learn the gob-smacking truth, though she's not aware of it.

211

Part of Nina's job is to stand by the coffin and talk about Grandad. She's been at Grandma's, learned stuff about his life. When the music stops, she starts to speak.

'We're here this morning to celebrate the life of John Lee. You who have known John, know that he wouldn't want you to be . . .'

I'm not listening, not really. It's my first funeral, and I can't stop staring at the coffin. *Grandad's in there*. It's heaped with flowers he can't see, and everybody heard his favourite music except him. I'm holding Mum's hand, breathing round a big aching lump in my throat, trying not to cry. If I cry it'll start Mum off. Nina's voice seems to come from a long way off.

'– or Jack, as he preferred to be called, spent three years during the nineteen fifties at Cold Tarn Open Air School, an institution which no longer exists.'

Jack. My heart kicks me in the ribs, my hand tightens on Mum's. She glances at me, whispers. 'What is it, sweetheart?'

I shake my head, staring at the coffin. 'It's . . . *Jack*,' I gasp. 'Jack, who looked after me when I was . . . in the nick of time. He's *Grandad*. I mean,

Grandad used to be *him*.' I shake my head. 'I don't know *what* I mean, Mum.'

Mum stands up, we're causing a disturbance. Outside we find a bench. She looks at me intently. 'Your grandad,' she murmurs, 'at the hospital, said something about the nick of time. *We're together in the nick of time*. We were talking about you and him. I thought it was the morphine . . .'

'No.' I shake my head. 'He was *there*, Mum, in the nick of time. He was my friend. Without him, I wouldn't be here now.'

A shaft of sunlight scores a direct hit on a splash of yellow crocus. She smiles, gazing at it.

'The same goes for me,' she says.

ABOMINATION
Robert Swindells

Martha is twelve – and very different from other kids, because of her parents. Strict members of a religious group – the Brethren – their rules dominate Martha's life. And one rule is the most important of all: she must never ever invite anyone home. If she does, their shameful secret – Abomination – could be revealed. But as Martha makes her first real friend in Scott, a new boy at school, she begins to wonder. Is she doing the right thing by helping to keep Abomination a secret? And just how far will her parents go to prevent the truth from being known?

'A TAUT AND THRILLING NOVEL FROM A MASTER OF THE UNPREDICTABLE'
Daily Telegraph

Shortlisted for the Whitbread Award

Winner of the Sheffield Children's Book Award

978 0 552 55588 3

CORGI BOOKS

BLITZED
Robert Swindells

Imagine being alive before your parents were
even born!

George is fascinated by World War Two – bombers,
Nazis, doodlebugs. Even evacuation and rationing
has got to be more exciting than living in dreary
old Witchfield! He is looking forward to his school
trip to Eden Camp, a World War Two museum.
But he doesn't realize quite how authentic this
visit to wartime Britain will be . . .

A hand reaching out of the fake rubble, a slip in
time, and George has to survive something much
worse than boredom. The rubble is now real –
he has slipped though time into 1940s London!

A THRILLING DRAMA FROM A MASTER OF
SUSPENSE, ROBERT SWINDELLS

978 0 552 55589 0

CORGI BOOKS

TIMESNATCH
Robert Swindells

Once a creature is extinct, it's gone for ever, isn't it?

Not any more – as a butterfly from the past proves.
The physicist mother of Kizzy Rye and Fraser Rye
has invented an amazing time machine that can
travel back into the past, snatch a plant or animal
now extinct and bring it back into the present.

It's a wonderful achievement, a real scientific
breakthrough. But the machine – 'Rye's Apparatus' –
has a horrifying potential. Suddenly Kizzy and
Fraser find themselves caught up in a terrifying spiral
of events – events that lead finally to a monstrous
demand from a sinister and violent organization.

Winner of the 1995 Earthworm Award,
7-11-year-old category

978 0 440 86227 0

CORGI BOOKS

NIGHTMARE STAIRS
Robert Swindells

I'm falling – falling down steep, narrow stairs – If I hit the bottom asleep, I know I'll never wake.

Every night Kirsty wakes up screaming. Every night she has the same terrible nightmare – of falling downstairs. But does she fall? Or is she pushed?

Then Kirsty discovers that her grandma died falling downstairs and she begins to wonder: is the dream hinting at a dark secret in her family? She has to know the truth. But tracking a murderer is a dangerous game, and as she delves into the past, Kirsty uncovers a secret more terrible than anything she can imagine.

A terrifying read from one of today's master storytellers.

Winner of the Sheffield Children's Book Award for Best Shorter Novel

'CLEVERLY PUT TOGETHER – FUNNY AS WELL AS GRIPPING'
Sunday Times

978 0 552 55590 6

CORGI BOOKS

INSIDE THE WORM and ROOM 13
Robert Swindells

INSIDE THE WORM
The worm was close now. So close Fliss could smell
the putrid stench of its breath. Its slavering jaws gaped
to engulf her . . .

Everyone in Elsworth knows the local legend about the
monstrous worm – or dragon – that once terrorised
the village. But it never really happened. Or did it?
For when Fliss and her friends are chosen to re-enact the
legend for the village Festival, the four who are to play
the part of the worm dance as one across the ground.
They are the worm. And Fliss begins to feel real fear.
Somehow the worm itself is returning – with a
thousand-year hunger in its belly, and a burning
desire for vengeance . . .

ROOM 13
Somebody was in there. Somebody – or some thing . . .

There is no room thirteen in the creepy Crow's Nest
Hotel, where Fliss and her friends are staying
on a school trip.

Or is there?

For at the stroke of midnight, something peculiar happens
to the door of the linen cupboard next to room 12.
And something is happening to Ellie-May Sunderland,
too – something very sinister . . .

A gripping page-turner from a master of spooky suspense,
award-winning Robert Swindells. Don't read this under
the covers at midnight!

Now available in a new omnibus edition

978 0 552 55591 3

CORGI BOOKS